Barren Earth

A Zombie/Science Fiction Novel By

Eric S. Brown
&
Stephen A. North

Artist: Jodi Lee

-Library of the Living Dead Press-

A "Library of the Living Dead" Book
Published by arrangement with the authors.

"Barren Earth"
By Eric S. Brown & Stephen A. North
Copyright 2009. All Rights Reserved

ISBN10- 1448636590
ISBN13- 9781448636594

This book is a work of fiction. People, places, events, and situation are the product of the author's imagination. Any resemblance to actual persons, living, dead or undead, or historical events, is purely coincidence. Except perhaps for that Pus fellow.

A Note From The Publisher

I've had the pleasure of working with both of the authors who wrote "Barren Earth". Library of the Living Dead Press began it's grand adventure in zombie land with Stephen A. North's "Dead Tide". Our second book was a collection of Eric S. Brown's best zombie short stories entitled "Unabridged, Unabashed & Undead". They are both great books and the authors are both dear friends of mine.

What you hold in your hands was a complete surprise to me. It seems that Stephen and Eric liked each other's writing styles so well, they figured it would make for a good project if they were to write together. What came about is a strange and wonderful mixture of zombies and science fiction. I call it "the undead and the unbelievable."

"Barren Earth" is like a chain letter gone horribly and perfectly crazy. One would write a chapter and send it via e-mail to the other. He would write and send it back. And so forth and so forth. What was born is a tale of the fantastic as well as a tale of horror.

You dear reader are about to enter the world of horror AND science fiction. Two genres for the price of one. Make sure you're strapped in tight. This is gonna be one helluva ride.

Undead love to you all,

Doc

2119 A.D.

Book One

The three people on the bridge all sat at their posts, still tense, even though the alarm klaxon was finally silent. Perhaps a kilometer away, the vast bulky remains of an alien warship drifted alongside theirs.

"Unknown vessel, this is Terran Federation Ship *Cormorant* requesting permission to board. Please identify yourself." The communications officer repeated the phrases for a fifth time, and then paused a moment to lick his dry lips.

"Might as well give it up Jackson, they aren't going to answer. That ship is a floating corpse." said the captain.

The younger man, Lt. Commander Neil Jackson, looked up from his console, "I know sir, but it is just hard to believe that we finally find evidence of other life, only to discover they're dead."

The captain nodded. "Even worse to discover that they died by violence." The image filling the view screen was too large at their current distance to see the entire ship. Magnification would have to be reduced. Right now huge, jagged holes were visible all over the other ship.

"Maybe there is life but it is just shielded from our sensors?"

The third person, Ensign Mary Powers, pointed to the strategic screen, just left of the main tactical display, "There's still a chance, Jackson. The second planet has a habitable atmosphere, and there is some sort of shielded facility on the second continent."

"And I'm picking up a transmission, sir!" said Jackson.

"A transmission, you say?" asked the captain.

"Yes sir."

"Powers, lay in a course to orbit the planet."

"Course set, Captain. Power readings are picking up from the planet. A planetary shield either just lowered or failed. Still no signs of biological life. There is a breathable atmosphere with gravity to our standards."

"What are the odds of that, eh?" The captain cocked his right elbow on the armrest of the chair, and rested his chin in his cupped palm. "Perhaps a robotic intelligence remains. We do appear to have an invitation to visit."

"We are within shuttle range now, Captain."

"Very well…" he said, then trailed off.

"Want me to put together a landing team, sir?" asked Jackson, looking at the older man.

"Don't see why not. If they were going to destroy us, they would have already. I don't believe there is any 'they,' because 'they' are dead. This whole system is dead. Can't you feel it? It feels like we're violating a tomb, but we must investigate. Go ahead, put together a team. Use bio-suits just in case, and take some Marines."

"Yes sir," Jackson replied, already on his feet.

Jackson

"*Cormorant*, are you getting the feed of this?" Jackson asked while settling the shuttle gently on a wide, tiled palazzo. They landed on the edge of a large ruined city complex bordered on three sides by what appeared to be impenetrable jungle and on the fourth, southern side by a large circular bay. "I'm sending Sergeant Marks, and Private Crane out first, then the rest of us will follow, over?"

"Reading you and seeing you loud and clear Jackson," said the voice of Ensign Powers. "Captain wants you to investigate source of transmission in large temple two clicks directly north of your position first, over."

"Affirmative, proceeding, out."

Jackson watched from the pilot's seat as the figures of Marks and Crane emerged from the shuttle's airlock and ran toward a low, crumbling stone wall that surrounded their landing zone.

Marks spoke, "All clear Commander. Nothing moving out here. But I'd swear we're being watched."

"Very good Sergeant. Stay alert. The rest of us are coming."

Jackson lifted himself up, out of the cockpit and onto the narrow slice of floor that separated the pilot seat from the co-pilot/navigator seat. It only took two steps to reach the ladder down into the passenger area, where Warrant Officer Leila Tran waited for him with the hood of her bio-suit pulled down. All the others were already outside.

"Here's your machine pistol, sir," she said with her faint

French accented English.

"Thanks," he said, unable to meet the woman's frank gaze. She only hid her feelings for him when others were around. He could never get used to someone loving him much as she did.

"You will be careful, Neil?"

"Yes Leila, and you be ready to come get us, if something happens."

He pulled her to his chest, inhaled the scent of her long, black hair and kissed her. Every bit of the pent up emotion he'd been holding back for the last day or so went into it. Then, a moment or two later, they parted.

"See you," he murmured into her ear.

Crane

They advanced in a long, spread out, v-shaped formation across a field of knee-high grass. A little breeze blew from the south, carrying with it a strange half-familiar scent of the sea. Each of them held a weapon, wore a protective suit that covered them from head to toe, and a helmet with a solar-sensitive visor.

Crane walked far out in front of the others, grumbling to himself. His finger fidgeted on the trigger guard of his short, stubby submachine gun. He was careful not to broadcast to anyone else, but felt the need to vent. Not even twenty feet away, five awkward-looking birds perched on top of the overturned wreck of some kind of tracked vehicle. None of them stirred. "Damn lazy things," Crane muttered, "must be the local version of vultures."

"You got that right," said someone nearby.

"Oh it's you Sola," he said to the small, tanned brown-haired woman a few feet away. She was recording the birds with her All-One, a scanner, recorder and sampling device about the size of a medium-sized purse. Her weapon was now slung over her shoulder. "Why did you break formation?"

"I'm a researcher," she replied, without turning around. "You do your job and I'll do mine."

"Bitch."

That one got her to turn around. Her delicate, beautiful little face was flushed with emotion. *Probably rage.*

"I heard that Crane."

"Your lack of discipline will get us killed."

"What is going on here?" thundered the voice of Sergeant Marks. He stopped walking right next to the tiny woman, forcing her to look up. He was over a foot taller than her five feet and a few inches. His assault rifle was pointed at the birds.

"Nothing Sergeant," Sola answered. "I just want to check out the wrecked vehicle. Get some shots of the local fauna."

Marks glared at her. "Use a little common sense, will you, Doctor? Those things are most likely predators. We're too close to them now."

She held up a hand, "You win Sergeant. I don't have the energy to argue with you. Let's skip it, eh?"

Marks nodded. "And get back to your place in the formation or I'll send you back to the shuttle."

Both men waited until she took her place, then Marks re-opened the radio channel, "Go ahead Crane, we don't have all day."

There wasn't a cloud in the sky as the breeze died away to nothing. The sun dominated the blasted landscape and the ruins of the dead city sprawling before them for kilometers. Six people, five straight backed, and one, hunched and misshapen toiled the final steps to top a small hill and stopped. A line of temples were the closest intact structures to them.

"This sun is torturing me, Botts," complained the tallest, a man named Tircek. Sweat was pouring off the man's raw-boned frame, staining his suit.

The hunch-backed man, beside him nodded, "Feels like we've been walking for hours.I wish we could take these damned suits off."

"I wish you would both stop complaining," said Sola. "Besides, it looks like we have found civilization."

"Civilization?" muttered the hunchback, "All I see is an open-aired tomb. Not a living soul down there, I bet."

" Probably plenty of *things*, though." Crane whispered to himself. He was close enough to the target structure to notice details. Much of the pyramid-shaped building was in ruins and sheathed with some sort of vine-like growth. Steps were visible ascending the west side of the building, but his orders were to make for the door that stood open at the base.

Last thing I want to do is go underground. Much rather climb.

He looked up at the violet-hued sky. The sun looked bigger than Sol. *I'm sure if I asked Tircek, he'd know if it was.*

"Stop beside the door, Crane," said Commander Jackson in his ear. "Wait for Marks to join you, then keep going."

"Yes sir," he answered, and noticed what looked like bones at the edge of the ramp that led down beneath the building. "Sir, I think I've found bones." *No doubt about it actually. I'm looking at a humanoid skull.*

The bones were scattered in the grass and had a scorched look, but what else could they be?

"Wait for the rest of us, then."

Moments later, they had a circular perimeter set up, and Jackson joined Crane where he found the bones. Both of them squatted in the grass, and Crane showed him the skull. Most of the cranium looked intact, and there were two holes where eye sockets should be. There was a jagged row of what looked like teeth, but the lower jaw and chin were missing.

"What are the odds Commander?" Crane asked.

"Impossible. These bones are ancient. None of our ships have been here before."

Jackson lifted the skull and placed it in a small opaque specimen bag. "Here Tircek, add this to your specimen bag."

Tircek stepped up. He handed Crane his shotgun, "Hold this a moment, will you?" he asked, then took off a backpack he wore. Jackson gave him the skull. A minute or two later, everything was stowed. He pulled the backpack back on, and took his shotgun back.

Guy's hands are huge. He could easily palm a basketball. Hell, maybe even a bowling ball!

"Want me to take point again, sir?" Crane asked. Jackson's visor was clear as a glass of water. The sky was getting darker.

"Yeah," Jackson said, and their eyes met briefly. "Do that."

Crane felt a chill then. It traveled up his arms and raised the hair on the back of his neck. He made himself stand up, and place his boots on the strange, spongy surface of the ramp. He took three steps down and flicked on the light in the top of his helmet. The walls had a raw fleshy look to them complete with rocky strands of what looked like gingeva.

I'm in a goddamned throat. Wonder if the rest of them feel it?

He wanted to look around, but didn't indulge the paranoid

desire. Something might leap out at him from the front. *Why worry about the people behind him?*

Twenty feet in, the rough-hewn passage leveled out.

The floor is smooth, at least.

He could see faint light through a doorway about fifty feet further in, He paused a moment, and looked back, taking a head count. Marks was right behind, followed by Jackson, then the medic Botts, and Tircek the geologist.

Where was Sola?

"Sola is missing. Anybody see anything?"

In the light of their headlamps several of his companions faceplates were completely transparent. He saw a gamut of emotions, but none apparently were feeling the panic coursing through him. *Except Jackson. He's as spooked as I am.*

He watched Jackson key his circuit for Sola, but couldn't hear anything. "Looks like we have some interference down here. No indirect communications. Not even with the shuttle or *Cormorant.*"

Marks pushed past Botts, heading back toward the entrance, "Bet she found some plant back there and doesn't even know we are gone."

"Now wait a minute," said Jackson, "we can't afford to split up."

"Well then, sir, why did we take any non-military types with us then? You know the way they are," said Marks.

"You are bordering on insubordination, Sergeant! We didn't

know what we'd run into down here."

"What do you suggest we do, sir? Do we wait for her to catch up?"

Crane wondered if maybe Sergeant Marks was a little edgier than he thought. *I'm definitely not enjoying this, and Jackson normally keeps it together pretty well, but not this time. Doesn't look like he has a clue what to do.*

"We will all go," said Jackson.

"There is a light ahead, Commander," said Tircek. "I'd like to check it out. It might be the source of the transmission."

"By yourself?"

"Sola will understand. Besides, my one gun wouldn't make much difference, would it?"

Jackson hesitated a moment longer, then said, "Crane stay with him."

Crane watched as the others turned to head back the way they had came in search of Sola. *Thanks a lot. Goddamn Sola. All that mattered to her was research. Now, I'm stuck down here with a giant freak.*

"Shall we proceed, Private Crane?" Tircek asked.

He sighed, "Yeah Doc, lets get this over with."

Sola

It was so easy to slip behind everyone. Tircek grinned at her, but said nothing. She liked him, but he was hard to know. Always kept to himself and refused to discuss his past. He'd talk all day about humanity's past, or linguistics, but nothing personal. Probably best to maintain distance anyway. Relationships equaled entanglements.

Nothing illustrated that better than her break-up with Dr. Norman Botts two days ago. He hadn't accepted the nature of their friendship well. Anyway, none of that mattered. What mattered was to get away from the overprotective gaze of Jackson and the two soldiers.

The moment Tircek turned his attention away, she slipped back up the passage. Odds were good that they wouldn't even miss her. Still, every moment counted. You only got one chance with Jackson.

Back at the entrance she settled the All-One carefully against her right hip and moved the strap to her left shoulder. Now she could brace it with her right and carry her pistol in her left.

She turned left, back onto the crumbling stone path, hyper-aware of her accelerated pulse. More of the birds were at the top of the temple above her, but she had enough footage on them for now. What she wanted was a closer look at some two and three story buildings a block or so further east.

Something smelled bad. The odor enveloped her as she reached the first of the buildings about a block away. A series of symbols were drawn on the wall's face just beside what appeared to be a door. No handles or buttons. The whole building was made of stone that glittered with mica. *Granite? Not my specialty.*

She stepped closer, still recording, but now also scanning the rock. Details of the building's composition began to scroll across her screen. Something about Muscovite Shist. *This was an important find! My insubordination is going to pay off!*

Data continued to spew across the screen. She took one more step and a cool breeze washed over her. Startled, she looked up. The door was open, but it was too dark inside to see anything. The stench freshened, apparently wafting from somewhere within.

The All-One had a light. She switched it on and played the beam across the opening. Something huge snarled and came straight for her. The dying afternoon sunlight played over a scaled hide, while the thing bared its fangs and took a swipe at her with a claw. The razor sharp talons cut right through her strap and the wrist that controlled the All-One. The piece of flesh and machinery flew free.

Sola staggered, blood fountaining from the ragged stump of her right hand. Too shocked to scream or even react, her back slammed against the wall behind her. The thing followed her out and scooped her up into its arms. Her vision faded in and out. She woke long enough, to see her hand still clutching the pistol in her lap, just as the thing carried her through the doorway.

Jackson

Jackson followed, taking the rear guard spot. Paranoia and a strong desire to see Leila again, gave him all the motivation he needed. Just seeing the sun was comforting as they emerged back outside.

"Anybody see Sola?" he asked.

"She's vanished sir," replied Marks,

Jackson looked back in the direction of the shuttle, but from here, all he could see were ruined buildings. He keyed his connection to the shuttle. "You still with us, Tran?"

"I'm here, Commander. Something wrong?"

"Not sure. Sola is missing. Keep an eye out for her, please."

"Yes sir."

"Anything around here to draw her attention?" asked Marks.

Out of the corner of his eye, Jackson noticed the hunched figure of Botts climbing the steps, or whatever they were, of the temple above them. He couldn't tell if they resembled Aztec, Mayan, or even Toltec ruins. He just knew they looked like the picture in his mind of them.

The top of the temple was about a hundred or so feet up. Botts kept climbing. Apparently he wasn't going to be any better at taking orders than Sola.

"Where are you going Botts?"

"Just thought the view might be better from up here, sir. Is that ok?"

"Ask next time."

Botts didn't even turn around.

"There's more of those birds up there, Botts," said Marks.

"I see them, Sergeant. My assault rifle is an excellent fowling piece."

The thought that keep turning over in Jackson's mind was that something knew they were here. Something lowered the planetary shields. The nature of it, dead, living, or robotic didn't really matter, just the intent. With Sola missing everything took on sinister connotations. He looked down what he took to be a street or avenue. Most of the stone was cracked or buckled. Few buildings looked intact. There were no skyscrapers like in a human city. Certainly nothing taller than this temple-type structure.

A block or so down a black object on the ground caught his attention.

"Marks, Botts, I think I see something."

Crane

Tircek had to lower his head to clear the doorway. He went in first, shotgun in hand, and stopped a few feet in. Over his shoulder, he said, "You smoke, Private?"

"Not really Doc, but why do you ask?" Crane answered, stopping beside the scientist. What he saw in the room, clenched his stomach, left him pasty-faced and nauseous.

"Cause I vote to take off these damn hoods at the least, and have a smoke."

From somewhere far away, Crane heard himself answer, "Commander Jackson won't like that."

Tircek raised an eyebrow at him. "Lotta things the commander doesn't like. Readings are all still checking out on my All-One. I can make some decisions for myself. Join me if you want." With that, the giant reached up and unfastened the seals around his neck and pulled the whole hood and helmet pieces off. His close-cropped blond hair looked sweaty and his pale face was flushed. "There, that's much better."

While the man fished around in a pouch fastened to his waist belt, Crane undid the seals on his mask and helmet. The air felt great on his skin. He could feel it drying the sweat almost immediately. *Thank God there was no smell.*

Tircek used a small tool to cut off the end of a cigar, then handed it to him.

The room was full of machinery, furniture that looked like it was made for humans, and what looked like shredded mummified remains. Some kind of last stand was fought here. Mixed in with the human remains were what looked like inch-long metallic flakes or scales. None of the cadavers were in good shape. This fight must have been savage.

"Light?" Tircek asked, with a lighter in hand. Crane leaned over, watched the flame, took a puff or two and then straightened up. Tircek put the lighter in the pouch on his waist.

"Nice aroma."

"I took the best I could get, some Cuban parejos, before we left. Save them for special occasions."

"You calling this a special occasion?"

Tircek inclined his head back and blew a perfect smoke ring. "I don't believe in parallel evolution, Private."

"Your suggesting that those are human corpses, then Doctor?"

"Terribly unprofessional of me, but yes, I am. Just don't know what happened yet. Too many questions."

Crane took a tentative puff. "All I know, is I want out. After being in the ship so long, being outside is great."

Tircek walked over toward the banks of machines and Crane trailed along behind him. Something was active here. The big man lowered himself carefully into a chair before a console of some sort. He reached over his shoulder and pulled his All-One from a sheath built into his backpack. He then attached a single earphone to his right ear. "This is the source of the signal, or transmission if you will," he said, indicating the console in front of him. "The language isn't one we know."

"I don't hear anything," said Crane, settling into a chair beside him.

"No, you wouldn't. The broadcast channel is higher than you can hear. Maybe the All-One can make something of it. It is the same message over and over, whatever it is."

"You can hear it, with that earplug or whatever it is?"

"I hear something, but I'm not sure what it is, yet. Here put this plug in your ear and hear for yourself."

Crane took the earphone. For a moment, there was nothing, then a sharp pain spiked through his head, static, distorted images flickering by, a voice speaking…The man's face was lined and old. He spoke, but the picture faded out. *The home worlds are all dead. Our enemy has defeated us, but we have in turn chased them across four solar systems. They fight to the last.*

More static… *and just like that all Hell broke loose in the jungle. All around us the vegetation parted and creatures like something straight out of nightmare charged. They were bipedal and humanoid in form but that was about all they had in common with humanity. Each of the things had four arms extending from their torsos and their skin was more like scales than flesh. Large, forked tongues dangled from their mouths as they hissed with fury at me and my people. It was clear they were hostile and I was left with no choice but to give the order. "Fire! Take them down!" I screamed at the top of my lungs, yanking my own gun from the holster on my hip. Our group's fire tore into the lizard-like savages with little effect. A few of the things that took heavier fire crumpled to the ground but most of them just kept coming despite the large holes blown in their bodies. "By all the Hells of Kreor!" I yelled as I placed close to dozen rounds in the lead creature and watched it keep coming without so much as flinching. It leapt onto me tearing at my armor with four sets of razor like talons and a mouthful of gleaming, metal like teeth. I screamed as the beast ripped my cuirass apart. I felt its filthy talons rake across my ribs as my blood sprayed onto the alien soil below the Aztarzs feet. Not far away, my friend Ulan lay dead while the creatures tore chunks of his flesh from his body and chewed with a series of sickening, smacking sounds.*

I pressed the muzzle of my gun against its head and pulled the trigger.

Lady Calyn and my brother Ellec carried me beneath a temple not far into the city. Therein, we made our last stand...

"Wake up Crane! Wake up!"

Jackson

He checked to make sure his weapon was off safe, then started a slow jog toward the distant object. Marks followed along, on the other side of the street, trailing by a few steps.

"Aren't we waiting for Botts, sir?" asked Marks.

"Nope! Dumb ass should be listening to orders. Tired of people ignoring me." He stumbled a bit on a loose piece of masonry. *Can hear myself breathing a little heavy. Need to spend more time in the gym, I guess.*

They ran past the rubble of two more houses, and slowed to a walk.

What looked like an All-One lay on the street, just past the still intact wall of a house. A hand, presumably Sola's still held onto the machine. The rest of her was hidden around the corner.

"Sola?" whispered Jackson, breathing a little hard.

No one answered.

Marks started forward.

"No, let me, Sergeant. She was my responsibility."

Behind them, the sound of Botts labored breathing and clattering boots drew closer.

Jackson edged up, then spun around the corner, submachine gun held braced against his hip.

Sola wasn't there. Just her hand, and a lot of blood. The red stain stood out against the bleached white stone, as if some sacrifice had been made.

Marks and Botts rounded the corner together.

"We have to get out of here," Jackson said. "We all go together to get Tircek and Crane and then we get the hell out of here."

"I'll second that," said Botts.

Crane

"We have the information, Crane! Wake up!"

The voice finally got through. Crane realized he'd been ignoring it.

"Ok, Doc, I'm back with you. I was actually living some guy's final moments, there."

Tircek had a strange look on his face. "Unless you want to repeat that experience, we need to leave now, Private!"

Crane scrambled to his feet, grabbing his weapon on the way up. Tircek was already turning away from him, heading for the doorway.

A bestial snarl outside in the passage caused both men to stop. Tircek lifted his shotgun, fitting the folding stock against his shoulder. *Thank God he's with me and not Botts.*

Can't move.

An awful smell of rot swept into the room. Standing framed in the doorway was one of the creatures. The head was bulbous on top, with a single eye on a segmented stalk, set just above a maw of serrated teeth. The eye retreated under a heavy brow, as the thing stepped closer. There were four arms, each ending with three finger talons, a barrel chest, and two legs.

Crane panicked. The submachine gun jerked in his hands as he squeezed the trigger. The extended burst climbed from the bottom of the creature's torso right to the top of its skull and into the ceiling, the bullets impact parting scales and flesh like putty. He fired until the magazine ran dry. His ears rang from the weapon's echoing roar.

"Calm down, Private. Better re-load before we go any further."

Crane heard himself whimper. "Never killed anything before, Doc. Couldn't help it."

"Better get a grip soon, son. Panic will get us both killed for sure."

The bigger man stepped past Crane, and over the corpse, while Crane re-loaded. He tossed the empty magazine into a cargo pocket on his pants, and pulled a fresh one from the ammo pouch on his belt. *Fresh fifty rounds. I better not waste this one. Wonder why this guy isn't scared? Since when do scientists have nerves of steel?*

"Sure you don't want me to go first, Doctor?" he asked.

The doctor turned around, briefly, "Hell yes, I want you to go first. I don't need an itchy trigger finger behind me!"

Ouch!

"Guess I deserved that. I feel better now. The shakes are gone."

"Ok, then do your thing, Private, and I'll cover the retreat."

Crane pushed past and hurried up the passage, back toward the light and open sky.

Jackson

They all ran.

"You should have grabbed Sola's All-One, I said!" said Botts. Even through the visor, his face was visibly red, and his hair stringy from sweat. The flush at each of his cheeks looked unhealthy. None of them were in very good shape. *Too much time in a starship.*

"There was no time," snapped Marks.

"Her death is for nothing without her research. Isn't that worth anything to you Commander?"

Jackson shrugged. "Chance we all take, Doctor."

"She might not even be dead. With her All-One we could be sure."

"If it wasn't broken," said Marks.

The hunchbacked man glared at the soldier. Other than the hunch caused by a curved spine, he was completely normal, even good-looking. *No weakling either. The guy's got a pair of arms and shoulders on him.*

"I'm going back for it, whether you two come or not," Botts said.

Marks snorted, and looked over at Jackson. "You going to let this egghead dictate to us, sir?"

Jackson thought about it. The scientist had a point. Everything was for nothing if they returned to *Cormorant* without any records. "Ok, Doctor, we go back for the All-One, and then you do what you're told until we get back to the ship."

Botts might have grinned, but Jackson couldn't be sure. The other man was already running back the way they came.

Jackson and Marks followed, but not with as much enthusiasm. Both of them actually slowed to a walk as Botts increased the distance between them. The civilian was over a block ahead when he reached Sola's All-One. Both men watched in shock as he picked up her hand and put it into a sample bag. He then turned around and started a slow jog back to them.

"These people got no instinct for self-preservation, sir. Sooner we're off this rock, the happier I'll be."

"Guess that single-mindedness comes in handy when they need to focus, Sergeant, but it does suck to look out for them."

Marks grinned.

In the sergeant's eyes, Jackson knew, he was barely military himself, just a damn Communication Officer. The stories still floated around the ship about when Jackson was the Recruiting Officer for the 2nd Fleet on Tiberius Twelve, otherwise known as Tiberius Brown's planet. They all knew he had balls and having the respect of soldiers was important to him.

"You know sir, for a borderline civilian, you really aren't a bad guy."

"We get grunt training , Marks. I just went on to better things. If we had to, I could probably call down an orbital barrage. Can you say the same?"

Marks shook his head. "That's part of the training I'll get at the Advanced NCO school on Bacchus Two."

"That one of those hell planets that barely support life?"

"It ain't a vacation hotspot."

Just then, Botts caught up to them, and all three started a slow jog toward the temple.

"Can't believe you picked up her hand," said Marks.

"There is sure to be some sort of evidence, perhaps even biological as to what severed her hand. Being thorough is vital to accuracy."

"You soulless fuck!"

Marks trailed off as they all saw Tircek and Crane back out of the temple, guns blazing.

"Hurry," Jackson said, taking a ragged breath.

Something followed Tircek up and out of the passage, despite two blasts from his shotgun, as Crane tripped and sprawled on the ground behind Tircek. The bigger man trampled him in his haste to get out of the range of the rampaging creature following them.

Talons ripped across Tircek's left thigh, and he fell, finger pressing down on the trigger of his weapon. Five or six shots from the shotgun literally ripped the four-armed scaly thing apart. A good portion of its torso vanished along with the top of its head. The remains splattered over Crane.

Crane stood up, with violet ichor spattered all over his back. Tircek fired once more and apparently needed to re-load. Two more of the creatures sprang from the tunnel and grabbed Crane. Tircek stumbled backwards as Crane fell face first.

"Fall back!" Marks ordered. "Head for the shuttle!"

"Negative on that!" Jackson's said over the comlink in his helmet. "They have us cut-off. Follow me!"

To his credit, Tircek didn't abandon Crane. The big man tossed the empty shotgun aside and waded into the creatures, striking out with his ham-sized fists. At his feet, Crane writhed in agony as the two creatures tore him apart. His left arm and leg were already severed, and Jackson caught a glimpse of his haggard face just as one of the creatures snapped its jaws closed. A primed grenade popped free from Crane's right hand and rolled two inches.

"Tircek run!" shouted Botts, apparently seeing the same thing Jackson did.

Tircek ignored him and instead grabbed the head of the second creature and shoved his fingers its eyes.

The grenade went off. Most of Crane and his killer simply vanished, while Tircek and his adversary caught the rest of the blast. Both of them flew a short distance and landed without grace in a boneless sprawl.

More creatures poured out of the tunnel and saw the three survivors almost immediately.

Jackson panicked. *What are we doing just standing here watching our shipmates die?* He forced himself into action. "They're coming for us! On the double, let's go!"

Roars and enraged snarls followed them as they ran through the ruins. Jackson tried to focus on the map scrolling across the interior of his visor. "Tran can you hear me?"

"Yes sir! I've been monitoring all channels. Ready to be

picked up?"

"Yes! Can you see the location on my visor mapboard?"

"Looks like a small hill inside the jungle."

"That's right! We are close to the city's fringe now. I estimate we will be at that location in less than five minutes."

"I'll be there, sir!"

"Good, Jackson out!"

"Tran out."

Jackson jumped a low wall and felt the spring of coiled grass under his boots. He sprinted through the jungle, firing at the monsters that were closing in on them.

Botts and Marks were right behind him, as the shuttle streaked through the sky above. The whine of its engine was deafening even inside his suit as Jackson took stock of the situation. Half of his team were missing, taken by the lizard things. Marks was already hoping aboard the shuttle which had barely hit the ground , its bay door already open. Botts raced past and threw himself inside the ship. Jackson stopped, bracing himself in the doorway. One more look around, and he spotted Tircek limping after them. He had his gun and Crane's. *How did he get away? Maybe the things had had enough?*

The creatures did seem to be standing off.

A moment or two later, Jackson helped Tircek swing aboard and then he closed the hatch. As soon as he did, the shuttle lifted off at full power. It shot upwards into the sky back towards the *Cormorant*. All of them crowded together on two benches.

Too many lost for nothing Jackson thought. *Even two is too many.*

"Did you see those things?" Tircek said to him with wide eyes. "They were rotting."

"What?" Jackson asked. Things had happened so fast, it had been hard for him to see much beyond the fact that monsters were alien and lizard like.

"Their scales. . . their wounds," Tircek informed him. "We didn't do all that damage. They were dead already when they came at us."

"You're crazy man," Marks said.

"Our bullets didn't even faze them," Tircek continued on as if he were talking to himself, completely ignoring Marks. "It was as if they couldn't feel a thing we did to them even when we shot their limbs clean off, they just kept coming."

Marks stared at Tircek. "Uh sir. . . Your bio-suit has a tear in it," he said as the shuttle landed aboard the *Cormorant.*

Tircek sighed, looking down at his wounded thigh, "No worries, Sergeant, I am sure our decon protocols will catch anything that might be a danger. I was lucky that alien absorbed the worst of the grenade for me, although I am almost deaf now."

Jackson thought of the lizard things below and shuddered. "I hope so Doctor," he said sincerely, "I certainly hope so." At least their mission was over and they were headed home. Jackson was going to be very happy to get away from the rest of crew. They'd been stuck together, out here in space, far too long.

All except him and Leila. Might have to replace a few bad moments in my mind, yes, indeed.

.

2122 A.D.

Peter

Peter kicked off the floor floating up the work shaft towards the *Hyperion's* engine room. The repairs had gone smoothly. After five years in deep space, the ship was holding up remarkably well. He supposed he could take more than a little credit for that fact. Peter smiled as he neared the top of the shaft and reached out taking hold of the access ladder. He positioned himself on it and said "Gravity on." Climbing the last few feet, he pulled himself up into the engine room. Claudia was waiting on him.

"Do you always have to do that?" she asked with a grin, the grin that always stopped his heart for a beat or two.

Peter laughed. "What's the point of being in space if you don't get to fly from time to time?"

"You're standing a little close, aren't you mister?" A lock of her long blond hair fell over her left eye as she looked up at him.

"Not close enough," he said, while reaching out and pulling her close. He leaned down for a kiss, feeling his blood race. Their lips met briefly, and he ran a hand down her back. She pulled away, putting distance between them.

At least this time she's still smiling. Am I forgiven?

"The captain wants to see you," she informed him. "He wants to know if everything is ready for the leap home."

Peter shook his head. "Earth, I still can't believe we're headed back already. Where did the years go?"

"Maybe you aren't ready to go back."

"Not sure. Thank god the mission was a success."

Her smile faltered. "You ever going to let your grudge against the captain, go? Things may not be so rosy for you soon. Why chance throwing twelve years away? You could end up an Engineer's Mate on a tramp ship to a convict planet."

"Probably more what I'm suited for. We made things work, but you know I'll never see eye to eye with him. God knows I never expected to be a Fletcher Christian on the goddamned Bounty, and I can never forgive myself for siding with him."

"I'm sorry, Peter…"

Reach out. Now! Here's your chance.

He ignored the voice. "What gets me, Claudia, is that he never even realized how the whole crew felt. I'll go see what he wants."

Might have been my last chance.

Edwards

Captain Edwards looked up from the logs he was going through as Peter entered his workroom.

"Heard you wanted to see me?"

Edwards scowled at the engineer. Five years aboard one of the most advanced ships in the fleet, under his own tight reign, hadn't diminished the man's casual attitude in the slightest. "Take a seat, Hoyle," Edwards gestured across his desk towards the chair opposite from him. Peter plopped into it.

"Is she ready for the leap?"

"All systems are go. She just needs another half hour or so to finish powering up."

"Good," Edwards nodded.

The *Hyperion* was massive, built to explore beyond the borders of known space. She was a cross between a science vessel and a heavy warship. Shaped like a strange looking cruise missile, she was 850 meters long and contained numerous decks as well as a fighter/shuttle bay. Most of her space was empty now and the large stock piles of supplies depleted from her long voyage. Her hull had once been covered with a wide of array of sensor modules and communications arrays but they were gone.. The gray metal of her exterior armor showed the trauma she'd suffered a year before from emerging too close from one of her leaps to a small star. By a miracle, she'd managed to build power and leap away again before her nine monster-sized real space engines burnt out and she'd was pulled into the giant fusion reactor by its gravity well. Still she had suffered a lot of damage. Most of primary systems were easily brought back online and her leap drive was functional enough to keep her moving and get her home. She was presently back inside known space and within a single short leap of Earth. Edwards hated being out of touch with Earth Command. He presumed they'd long ago written off the Hyperion as lost. He and his crew had received their last communiqué from Earth Command over a year and a half ago and it was time delayed by the lag of traveling through real space. No one had invented a means of sending signals through the void of leap space yet. That kind of instantaneous, real time communication still belonged to the realm of science fiction if you were more than an AU apart. Now they were in range though but with no equipment to send or receive a message. Command was going to be in for a quite a shock when they dropped out of leap space into Earth orbit. The short range comm. Gear of the shuttles and fighters still worked so Edwards plan was to promptly launch a shuttle and establish a channel to Earth Command before they were taken as hostile and fired upon. It was risky but it was his only option. Besides, Earth's sensors would instantly recognize the *Hyperion* as she appeared but Edwards always liked to look on the dark side of things and the worst case scenario. The other forty nine members of his crew had learned to be thankful for his over cautiousness during their long trip. His dark zealousness had saved the ship more than once.

"Forget one more time to address me properly Hoyle. Just once more."

"Sorry about that, *sir*."

"You presume too much. I want you on the shuttle and pick four good people to go with you."

"How about Claudia Coyne, Garrett Fergusson, Janet Donner, and Frank Litz?"

"Good. Let me know the minute the drive's charged," Edwards ordered Peter and turned his attention back to reviewing the ship's logs so they'd be ready for his debriefing upon their arrival. Peter nodded and hurried from the room.

Peter

Can't get past this bad feeling. Why dread going home?
Peter wondered.

As the seconds ticked by until the leap commenced. the initial vibration of the drive engaged. It was a feeling he'd never get used to it: the sudden gut-wrenching sensation of falling forwards; the sound of an angel chorus, droning up and down the scale. Impossible to guess how long, but the leaps always seemed to last forever. Outside the *Hyperion* the stars disappeared and the whole of existence became filled with the blood red nothingness of leap space. Then with the blink of an eye the mighty ship dropped back into our reality above the Earth. The shield which served as the shuttle bay door flickered out and Peter leaned back in the pilot chair of the shuttle. He spoke into his helmet microphone, "This is shuttle Alpha 2-9. We're leaving the bay now. All systems go." Glanced briefly over at Claudia beside him. *Her eyes are already closed. Looks tense. We all are.*

Edwards didn't reply.

As the engines of the *Hyperion's* leap drive powered down, and with only a slight hesitation, Peter fired the shuttle's thrusters, quickly gained lift and speed, and exited the shuttle bay. *Hyperion's* bulk was to their left, and there glittering below them was an orb of vibrant blues and greens shining beautifully in the blackness surrounding it. Earth. Home.

Claudia's voice beside him, "*Hyperion* Shuttle Two-Nine to Earth Command, over?"

No one answered..

"Luna Central, do you read me? Orbital Command?" Peter listened to her try these and other separate stations without response.

The door behind them, to the passenger cabin, opened. Garrett poked his head in, "We having problems?"

Peter said, over his shoulder, "No response from any station."

"Peter," Claudia said, her voice filled with urgency. Peter spun around in his seat. "What is it?"

"I've got four fighters inbound on an intercept course."

Peter took a glance at the sensor data himself. "What the...?"

The shuttle's database couldn't identify the make of the fighters. They had the same sleek manta shape of the Hades Class, but appeared to have been reconfigured. Their engines were burning hot as if their radiation scrubbers were off-line.

This didn't make any sense. If Earth Command truly saw the Hyperion as hostile or a threat of some kind, they'd be dust by now so why did the fighters all have their weapons locked on them?

"I'm getting a message," Claudia informed him. She punched a few keys on her station's console and a hollow, gravely voice filled the pilot's compartment. "Welcome home crew of the *Hyperion*. I wish we could say we'd been expecting you," it rasped. "Please recall your shuttle. You'll be boarded shortly. A Decon. Vessel is already in route to your position."

"This *Hyperion* shuttle Alpha 2-9. The Hyperion has taken damage. She has no communication capabilities at this time."

No reply came. Garrett who was still leaning into the front of the shuttle looked at Peter and Claudia. "Don't regulations require that we report to nearest space dock for decon and debriefing?"

Peter glared at Garrett knowing the man was right. "Earth Command did you say a decon ship is in route to us?"

"Much has changed in your time away Alpha 2-9. All ships are now boarded for inspection and preliminary decontamination before being allowed to dock with any orbital facility. Your communication problems are understood. Please return to the *Hyperion* and prepare to be boarded."

"Yes sir," Peter answered curtly.

"Well, that's certainly weird," Garrett commented.

Most of the *Hyperion's* crew gathered in the spacious hangar outside the docking/launching area of the ship's shuttle bay. Peter's news of the Hyperion being boarded traveled fast. Everyone not at a crucial post wanted to be there to meet their guests. They'd all been in space a long time and were eager to catch up on what happened on Earth while they were away. Captain Edwards, Peter, and Garrett stood at the front of the crowd.

Peter glanced toward Claudia where she stood in the last rank of crewmen. Just behind her was the entrance to the Ready Room. She gave him a small smile. Peter's bad feeling lingered still and Garrett was clearly on edge. As the ranking officer of the small contingent of marines stationed on the ship, Garrett wore a sidearm on his hip and was the only armed member of the personnel present. No one but Peter took notice of the weapon but the engineer was glad Garrett carried it.

As the airlock to the docking area dilated open and the first of the "Decon" party stepped into the hangar, the crowd applauded and cheered. His presence meant they'd made it. They were really home at last. The Decon officer wore a full body biosuit which looked like jet black armor covering him from head to toe. His features were invisible behind the suit's sleek faceplate which was as black as the rest of the armor. He carried a kit of some kind of gear in his right hand. Six more Decon squad members followed him. Each of them was armed with what looked like modified combat shotguns. *But modified how? Ah, I think it is an expanded magazine.*

Captain Edwards stepped forward to meet the officer with the kit. "What's the meaning of this? Why are you armed?" the captain demanded.

"Calm yourself," the officer said holding a hand out towards the captain warning him to stay back. "The Earth is at war. This ship will be inspected for alien pathogens and other threats to the security of the planet. If you resist, I have the authority to order you shot."

Edwards' face went white at the officer's threat. The entire hangar fell silent. While everyone else was fixated on the confrontation between Edwards and the Decon officer, Peter felt Garrett give him a nudge. The Decon squad spread out, flanking the crowd, as if they were finding better firing positions. *This can't be happening. There has to be an explanation.* Garrett leaned in close, "Be ready," he whispered. Peter shot him a glance back wondering what he was supposed to be ready for.

Edwards still stood frozen, probably waiting to find out how the Decon process was going to be carried out, when the voice underneath the faceplate barked, "Take them!"

All six of the armed squad members opened up at once. Their weapons thundered again and again as they dropped one target and moved on to the next. Peter watched the captain go down, a large needle like projectile sticking out from his chest. The hangar erupted into a panicked chaos of screams and gunshots. He looked for Garrett but the marine leader was already on the floor. His gun lay a few feet from him as if it had been flung from his hand as he'd tried to draw it but was struck before he could bring it into play. Peter jumped for the weapon. He hit the floor snatching it up and rolled back to his feet. Half of the gathered crew were already down. No sign of Claudia, though. He ducked into the moving mass of those who remained standing, trying to make his way through them to the hangar's exit, the Ready Room. Nothing he could do would help the others. One man with a single pistol couldn't make a stand against seven armed people in bio-armor. His only hope was to make it out and warn anyone who hadn't came to the hangar to meet the Decon squad. *And find Claudia. Oh God, if they killed her.* Maybe, if God was with them, they could deal with the boarding party and get the Hyperion the hell out of here before more were given a chance to come aboard. He didn't know exactly how many of the crew stayed at their posts but he guessed it to be at least a dozen. Frank was probably on the bridge. He and Claudia weren't much higher on Edward's list than he was.

People cried out and fell all around him: White uniformed figures, smeared crimson, some friends, all of them familiar, falling, screaming. Suddenly, living long enough to get out of this room was going to be a tall order.

The crowd was thinning out behind him as he reached the Ready Room and almost fell through the door. *I know all of these people.* Two or three bodies sprawled in the room beyond, near the row of benches and the long line of lockers. Two of them were his men, and the third facedown with a needle in her back...a woman with long blond hair.

"Claudia!" he screamed.

A hand grabbed his shoulder, and he spun, barely aware of the hate contorting his face, and the snarl that issued from his lips. *One of the Decon soldiers!* Without hesitation he pressed the pistol up against the man's faceplate and fired. Liquified bone and brain splattered across Peter's face, chest and arms. The horrible stench of putrified flesh filled his nose, cloying and overpowering.

The corpse sagged backwards and he helped it along with a shove.

For the moment, he shared the room with only the dead.

No way Claudia is still alive! But I must be sure!

He knelt down, and with a clumsy hand, felt for a pulse in her neck. As his fingers touched her skin, she moaned. *Thank God!*

"Hang in there babe, just hold on. I'm with you." He lifted her without removing the needle. *Better to leave it there for now.* He started to run, the pistol still in his right hand as he cradled her in his arms. Blood ran from the edge of her mouth. So much blood. Red light strobed over them both as he stepped into the passage and turned left. The alarm sirens drowned out the sound of his sobbing breath and pounding boots.

Got to reach the escape pod! The onboard robodoc will save her!

Frank

He sat paralyzed in the command chair, listening to the screams, the gunfire, and then a short interval of silence. Each time a new situation confronts him, he hesitates, but the delay has shortened. Quite a bit actually since the beginning of the voyage. Of course, most people think he is just slow. *Poor Frank, befuddled again.*

Nothing could be farther than the truth. He looked up at the three screens across the room from him. The third from the left was what they called the tactical view. The symbols for the immense bulk of a heavy cruiser and an escort carrier were now present, roughly forty miles from *Hyperion*. A cloud of lesser ships, probably more fighters and perhaps shuttles were halfway to the *Hyperion*. The names of the two ships appeared above the symbols: The heavy cruiser was the *Julio Cesare* and the escort carrier was the *Roma*. *That's strange. Both of those ships were in the process of being decommissioned years ago.*

Doesn't look good. Most of *Hyperion's* weapons systems could be operated independently of human control, but all of the current targets were identified as friendly. *Have to change the targeting parameters now!* The menu was right there beneath his fingertips. *But almost everyone is dead!* The middle screen, on the wall, currently showed the ship's interior, overhead, deck by deck. A flick of his finger cycled through each one. All surviving personnel were identified and highlighted. Hostiles were outlined in red.

The hostiles now out-numbered the survivors.

Not going to win the battle within or without. Need to gather anybody I can and get the hell off ship!

Frank paused a final time. Three survivors were making for the escape pod on Deck Three. At least that was what he surmised. Nothing else was there. One last look at the screens and a quick stop by the drop shaft door at the arms locker. Nothing heavy like a rifle in there, unfortunately, but there are two specialized shotgun pistols, both equipped with 10 round drum magazines. He took the pistols and a handful of loaded magazines.

With a pistol in either hand, he stopped by the door, waited for it to slide open, then stepped out into the shaft. "Gravity on," he said, and fell like a stone in a deep well.

A moment or two later, he said, "Gravity off," and felt the abrupt shift drag him to an immediate halt, almost exactly even with the ladder rungs and the door to Deck Three.

Such a fall may have greatly injured a human but Frank's body was built to withstand far greater impacts. Reached out, guns still drawn, and hooked his hands through the rungs, pulling himself toward the door. The panel slid to the side into the wall, and he exited onto the main passage that ran the length of the ship.

Frank almost ran into the backs of two Decon Soldiers. As it was, they were turning toward him as he ran at them firing both pistols, point blank. One soldier took a shot square in the chest and another in the neck. The second took two shots to the groin and collapsed against the wall. At near point blank range, the heavy solid slugs tore them both to pieces, leaving huge gaping wounds despite their armor. Frank plunged right past them, continuing to fire as the two men refuse to stay down! Two shots from a Laymon Hand Cannon were usually more than enough to put down an elephant.

The guy with the groin shot, on the right, had a grip on his rifle, and swung it around. Frank fired twice more and the man's head disintegrated in a welter of blood, bone, and maggots. A terrible rotten egg stench filled the air, and Frank spun on his heels toward the other man. He fired twice more with the left hand gun, aware only of an explosion of foul black gore and ivory white bone.

He kept running, jumping over the humanoid-shaped remains of a security bot.

Almost there! The next right…

More soldiers! Where'd they come from?

Worst of all, right in front of the pod's entrance lay the bodies of Peter and Claudia. And then, there were three soldiers with slug rifles centered on his chest.

The soldier on the left sneered, and said, "Drop the guns and live. We will spare the lives of these others if you do."

Frank dropped the guns.

"Now, empty your pockets!"

Frank dropped the extra magazines of ammo beside the guns. The soldier motioned him to step back, then reached down and picked everything up.

Peter and Claudia's bodies were gathered up and Frank was led by a new squad of Decon soldiers to the hanger bay. There were now five shuttles docked aboard the Hyperion. Frank watched as his friends were loaded like meat into one of the ships.

"Human, you have no idea how lucky you are," purred the commander for the Decon personnel. "We needed some prisoners. If it wasn't for what you and your friends know about this ship and its mission, I would frag you right now. Get onto the shuttle. You'll be flying up front with me where I can keep an eye you on. Go ahead and place the woman in the robodoc."

The shuttle sealed its door. Its configuration was far different than the shuttles of the Hyperion or any human shuttle Frank could remember traveling on since his creation. The temperature was far colder than most humans preferred it. He noticed none of the Decon squad removed their armor.

Frank took a seat in the large pilot's area with the commander, the pilot, and two armed guards. Peter was still back watching over Claudia while she was in the robodoc. One of the guards stood and both of them kept their weapons ready should he try anything. The shuttle's engines roared to life and the craft left the Hyperion for the blackness of space. "This is cargo Shuttle 3 requesting permission to enter Earth atmosphere with prisoners on board."

"Permission granted Shuttle 3. What is your destination?"

"We are in route to New York, the science center of Dr. Gallows. ETA- fifteen minutes."

"Understood Shuttle 3."

Frank watched the fiery rage of Earth's atmosphere burning over the shuttle's forward window as it dove downwards. It broke through the clouds into open air, with the city of New York far below. Frank peered out the window, watched every detail emerge as they drew closer. New York had changed. Gone were the glittering towers of humanity and the bright lights. Instead, the city sprawling out below them looked as if a war had destroyed it and was only now being rebuilt. Dark, spear like towers rose to touch the gray clouds of the sky. Great swathes of the original city appeared to be underwater. The shuttle landed on a platform of one of the few remaining original buildings and Frank disembarked with his guards leading the way.

I wonder if the sky is always gray, now?

The guard who took his pistols, a hulking man with peeling skin, kicked Peter and Claudia. "Get up, up or we will turn you over to the Beasts!"

Peter scrambled to his feet and helped Claudia up. Her face was gray, but she managed to stand with Peter's arm around her. Both of them were herded out of the ship to stand near Frank.

"Beasts?" Peter asked.

"I'm sure you will find out on your own," said one of the guards.

On a nearby platform a second shuttle disgorged its passengers.

"That's our crew," said Claudia.

"But how, I even see the Captain, and Fergusson. Aren't they dead? I'm sure they were." said Peter.

"You'll find out soon enough," the hulking guard growled.

Not long after, the guards herded them through an iris door and down a series of dimly lit passages. They passed several featureless doors. Without warning, or any instructions, the guards stopped at a door that looked like all the others.

"Open up 48 Jimmy," said the hulking guard to the smaller man beside him.

"Sure thing Vic." The smaller guard pointed something in his hand at a nearby door marked with the numerals 48, and the door opened. Vic pushed them all inside. "Relax while you can, meat," he said, "the end is near!"

"Meat?" asked Peter.

"That's what he said," said Claudia.

The room was small, with three bunks and a toilet.

Frank stood in front of them both, "I'll get you both out of here, if I can. It just may be tricky."

"Listen Frank," said Claudia, "I'm so sorry about the incident in the Virtual World, but..."

"Don't trouble yourself, Claudia. It doesn't matter. It never did."

He watched her eyes, then her mouth on that one.

"What do you mean? I know I hurt you. That Peter hurt you."

"I was confused and hurt until I understood. After that, it didn't matter."

Both Peter and Claudia stared at him. "That is a healthy attitude there," said Peter. "Gotta admit that you surprise me constantly. Had you pinned down as a dullard."

Frank grinned at him. "Funny, I always thought the same about you."

Claudia laughed, "He won that round Peter."

"Guess so."

Frank raised his hand, "You both look tired. Why don't both of you try to get some rest while I stand guard?"

"You mean that, Frank?" said Claudia.

"Yes, go ahead."

She did look tired. Within moments, he could tell they were both asleep.

Claudia

She fell, a headlong plunge, down into sleep, into a memory. Her wounds were only healed halfway, and she was so tired...

The wind blew restlessly in the trees. She was lost in the sweet grinding, rocking motion where their bodies met and merged. *So close...so close.*

She heard, felt a distant concussive boom and both of them looked up. In that instant, a wave of unreality washed over her and she could feel her body floating in womb-like darkness. The sun dimmed and complete confusion settled in. *Where am I?* Then, the light returned.

The man's handsome face was beneath her and their fingers were interlocked where she held his arms down against the earth. His eyes were a brilliant blue. The sweet dying sensation built and he whispered her name as they found release and their limbs convulsed.

"Claudia!" an anguished voice shouted, in the distance.

"Sounds like the cripple," he said.

Her anger rose right to the surface. "Don't call him that!"

"You want me to lie?"

"I want you to have some compassion."

"Goddamn it, Claudia, he is my friend too, but he is what he is. He takes twice as long to learn anything. I'd call that mentally crippled."

She shook her head, and levered herself up and away from him. He had an exasperated look on his face and his blue eyes were cold. *Wintry. Why didn't I ever notice that before?* "You are a bastard, Peter."

He gave her that lazy grin, full of mockery.

"Claudia!" The voice was closer, and there was nowhere to hide. Aside from the sleeping bag they were lying on, just leaves were underfoot, and the rotted remains of several fallen trees.

Where are my clothes ? She looked around, taking a step or two toward the nearby stream. *Ah, there*! *Right next to the stones.* She rushed to get dressed, knowing full well that Peter still hadn't moved.

Frank appeared near the stream, rounding a large boulder. She was still topless, bent over, with her panties just past her knees.

He didn't say anything: Just looked from her to Peter, then back again. His expression didn't change, and if anything he seemed…curious. Then, a moment later, he was gone, striding away into the trees.

Peter got to his feet finally, all the while watching her get dressed.

"That was strange," he said.

Yes it was.

The memory faded, just another incident, strange but not really remarkable, amid the adventures of their journey into space and back.

She slept.

El-ick

Admiral El-ick watched as the orb that was Alpha Centuri Prime came into view on the ship's forward screen. The Dreadnought, *Scar*, dropped out of leap space at his command only minutes before. Its sub-leap engines blazing on a course for the human world it was his task to destroy. He knew the task was impossible. So did Earth Command but missions like this were conducted every month to keep the accursed living from building a fleet of their own capable of threatening Earth. His real job was merely to weaken them and intimidate them into staying on their side of space until Earth Command finished assembling its armada to strike at the colonies, all of them, not just Alpha Centuri Prime, and end the human race for eternity. Two destroyers, the *Wound* and the *Maggot*, accompanied the *Scar* on this run. He smiled as he saw the five human battleships racing from the planet's orbit to intercept them. El-ick leaned back in his command chair and ran the tip of a finger down the smooth flesh of his nearly flawless face. His dark hair was ragged and unkempt but otherwise he looked the epitome of a conqueror. El-ick's body was lean and tight with muscles, enhanced by cybernetic filaments, under his gray uniform. His teeth were white and showed no imperfections.

El-ick's sharp green eyes were full of excitement as he spoke. "Have the *Wound* and the *Maggot* deal with the battleships. Put us on a course for the planet. Maximum thrust."

The human vessels opened up almost at the exact moment the destroyers launched their first waves of missiles. The space between the opposing ships filled with nukes burning towards their targets. "Countermeasures," El-ick ordered knowing the humans would've targeted *Scar* above the other two ships under his command. The *Scar* wasn't the flagship of the Earth's fleet but she was one of the largest and most advanced to ever have been constructed by rotting hands. Most of the ships in the Earth's fleet were older human vessels pulled from out of the mothballs but the number of ships like the ones under his command were growing. The dead worked around the clock trying not only to build their own but to make them better than the ones acquired from the remains of the extinct human civilization of the Earth. A pulse of energy sprang from the *Scar's* forward arrays rendering the bulk of the incoming, human missiles inert. The *Scar's* rail-guns took care of the rest as the massive dreadnought closed on the human fleet. *Maggot* was not so lucky. She took a nuke to her port side which tore a hole in her hull. If she had an atmosphere, it would be leaking into space. The dead rarely bothered with any form of life support on their warships beyond maintaining enough heat to keep them from freezing in the void of the stars. There was no point. They did not take prisoners. Three of the human vessels took severe damage from the exchange. One of them flared like an exploding star as it broke apart and ceased to exist. A second changed its course, veering hard to stern, in an attempt to flee before El-ick's fleet. The battle continued to rage around the *Scar* as El-ick eyed Centuri Prime. The humans no longer built their ships in space if at all possible. Space Docks were too vulnerable to attack without extreme orbital defenses like those around Earth so the humans built planet based shipyards instead. El-ick motioned at Dirk, his first officer. "Scan for the largest shipyard and turn it into a heap of slag and ashes."

"Yes sir!" Dirk nodded, his fingers dancing over the controls of his console. The *Scar's* 80 launch tubes spat nukes at the planet in a seemingly unending stream. One of the human destroyers spun from the battle racing the missiles towards the planet. El-ick watched as a dozen leap points flickered on the screen. More human ships had arrived to join the fight. Though the prospect of taking them all on appealed to him strongly, those were not his orders. "Order *Wound* and *Maggot* to recall their fighters! We've done enough here. Take us home!"

The three dead vessels flashed and disappeared from the space near Centuri Prime as the human battleship chasing the missiles aimed at the planet flew itself into their the nuke's path and vanished in a ball of flame, taking most of the strength of the attack with it, leaving only a handful to rain down upon the world. Within seconds, the mushroom clouds of nuclear detonation could be seen on the surface of the planet below.

Peter

When the guards came, all three of them were awake. Frank was leaning against a wall, and Peter and Claudia were sitting on a bunk.

There were three guards and a fourth man. Two of the guards were Vic and Jimmy. The third was someone new. They wore the familiar black bio-armor, and carried assault rifles.

The fourth man was about six feet tall with a medium build and wore a baggy brown jumpsuit. His pale skin, wherever it was visible, looked like it was covered in Vaseline, or something slimy or greasy. *Maybe suet?* Whatever the stuff was, it coated him, glistening on his high cheekbones and in his crew-cut hair.

"I'm Doctor Haiche, Doctor Gallows assistant. I'm here to take some tissue culture samples."

"When are we going to get some answers, Doctor?" asked Peter.

"You aren't, I'm afraid, Mr. Hoyle. Time is very short now, for you and your friends."

"Then why are we still alive? Why spare us?"

The doctor grinned, revealing a mouth full of enormous yellow teeth. "Well, as I've mentioned, the samples, and then you will provide some sport."

Haiche stepped close to Peter, holding some sort of instrument that just fit into his hand. "Let me see your arm."

Peter looked at Claudia, Frank, and then back to Haiche.

"We can do this two ways, Mr. Hoyle, the painless or the

painful, it is your choice for the moment." Haiche had a faint, supercilious smile on his face.

"Just give him your arm, Peter," said Claudia. "Get it over with."

Peter nodded, extending his arm toward Haiche.

The doctor ran the device over Peter's arm. A short, razor-sharp blade emerged. Without warning, he jabbed downward, gouging into the flesh of Peter's arm. Peter jerked, and threw himself backward, blood spraying.

Bastard! I'll get you for that!

The guard, Vic, started forward, gun pointed at Peter. Haiche raised a hand. "Leave him be."

Vic stopped, but frowned.

"Now you!" Haiche said while placing the bloody piece of Peter's flesh in a vial then stoppering it closed.

Claudia stepped forward, and stood still.

Her eyes were closed. Through the fabric of her suit the blade of the extractor tool passed across her belly. She swayed, shuddering as the cloth parted like tissue, revealing the smooth flesh beneath.

Peter stood still, feeling the sudden rush of blood to his cheeks, knowing his face was flushed. *Claudia!*

Vic was staring at him, hand on the big bore pistol. Peter could feel how bad the big man wanted to kill him.

Haiche's tool cut a path upward. Part of a pale breast appeared. The doctor slipped his hand inside...

Vic's hand pressed against his chest. Peter snarled, felt his adrenalin pulse and pound, and the gun was suddenly in his face.

"Do it, meat, come on. I want you to."

Haiche's arm jabbed and ripped free. Claudia cried out, falling away from him, but he fell with her. *He's actually laying on top of her! I can't actually stand here and watch this! Must do something! Do or die trying!*

Just then, Frank stirred to life, crossing quickly over toward the struggling couple. He grabbed the doctor's arm and twisted--- The man's arm broke and Frank caught the tool in mid-air. Incredibly, Haiche didn't make a sound, even as Frank reversed the tool in his hand and stabbed downward, burying the blade into his forehead.

Vic shouted, turning away from Peter, lifting the gun. The doctor's body flew through the air and knocked Vic down. Frank followed, bellowing his rage, and threw himself at the remaining two guards.

Now is my chance! Peter stepped over beside Vic. As the guard pushed the doctor's body away, he drove his boot heel down onto his face. And again. Felt bones break.

Again.

Vic was no longer moving. Peter reached down and pried the pistol out of the man's hand. Then he unfastened the belt from around the man's waist. All the while, he kept his eyes away from the gory spattered mess.

Two shots dragged his attention back to Frank. The other

man held a rifle in his trembling hands. One guard, Jimmy lay sprawled against the wall with a bloody red halo spattering the wall behind him, and the other lay face down on the floor. Both looked dead.

"Oh dear God, Peter, we have to get out of here," said Claudia.

"Here Peter," said Frank, "take a rifle."

Frank knelt down and unbuckled the pistol belt from Jimmy's waist. He picked up the other rifle. Checked it over. Watched Claudia pick up the third rifle.

"The way I see it," Claudia said, "is we either try to steal a shuttle or we get out of this building and into the city."

"The shuttle is the best option," Frank pointed out. "Let's go!"

Frank

Frank led the others through the winding corridors. The walls were gray and dull. It was very unlike those of the buildings he remembered from so long ago. It was a human trait to make things more colorful and life affirming. The lifeless colors disturbed him. He knew they couldn't fight their way out of this place. There was no way to know how large this building was or how many people resided in it. Up ahead he saw a terminal at the bend in the corridor. He motioned for Peter and Claudia to fall back and stay where they were. He approached it carefully, peering around the bend to make sure the area was clear. Once he saw it was safe he examined the terminal. He doubted it was tied into the main system of the building but still it could be useful. His fingers flew over it, calling up a stream of data which rolled across the screen at lightning speed. His eyes scanned the words as they flew past. He quickly memorized the layout of the building and the path to the shuttle docking area from where they were located. He also called up everything he could from the computer's limited knowledge of the Earth itself. Luck was with him and he was able to connect to the outside network via the terminal. Fresh information scrolled down the screen. For a moment, he couldn't bring himself to believe the things he was reading.

"Frank!" Claudia whispered at him, urging him to move on. He disengaged from the system and turned to his friends.

"We're in a lot of trouble," he remarked. "This way!" he ordered and darted on down the corridor. Peter closed in to match his pace and kept moving beside him.

"What is it?" Peter asked, "What did you find out?'

"The Earth is dead. Humanity as we know it died out years ago. A ship much like the Hyperion returned to Earth carrying a virus that killed everyone."

"What are you talking about? If everyone is dead, who were the guys we just killed?"

"They were dead Peter. I don't have time to explain. Just trust me that we need that shuttle and that escaping into the city will do us no good."

El-ick

El-ick sat behind the desk of his ready room which was adjacent to the bridge area of the SCAR. The door slid open as Dirk entered. El-ick looked up at him scowling. "What?"

"We just received new orders from Earth Command sir. They have requested we increase our speed and get home as fast as possible."

El-ick sat down the review of the ship's weapon upgrades he was working on. "Do it. Did they say why?'

"The *Hyperion* has just came home sir."

"The *Hyperion*?" El-ick asked. "The old Earth exploration vessel that was lost?"

Dirk nodded. "The crew was *alive.* They were taken prisoner by Earth Command for study and fresh bio samples for the food-clone vats."

"My lord," El-ick whispered to himself. "There are living humans on Earth again. If the colonies get word of this, they may try to hit us whether they're ready or not."

"I don't think they'll be able to sir. We hit them pretty hard on this run."

"Have you learned nothing about humans in all this time Dirk? They aren't exactly creatures of logic. The things we feel are but shadows of the emotions and passions that drive them. It's part of being alive. Emotion can be a powerful drive and throw things like logic and tactical readiness out the airlock in a situation like this."

El-ick stood up, heading for the bridge. "What our best ETA to Earth?"

"If we over burn the engines and risk damage, perhaps two hours."

"Make it sooner," El-ick ordered. "I want to see these *humans* myself before Earth Command hacks them up and hands them out in pieces and parts."

Claudia

She held the rifle ready and looked outside.

The landing pad was empty.

The sun was out, shining strongly against the blue sky and through puffy gray bellied clouds.

Just a sun-bleached stretch of concrete and steel awaited them. That, and a long drop to the ground below. *No way out this way, unless we're ready to end it all.*

The three of them stopped just under what appeared to be an air vent. A hot, humid breeze issued through the fragile rusting panels. The ramp to the pad was just feet away.

"Back to the stairs," said Peter, leading the way back to the door.

The concrete steps of the stairwell crumbled occasionally under their feet as they descended. Ten flights down, Claudia could feel sweat on her forehead. The walls were crusted with a pale fibrous material that broke away in chunks whenever one of them touched it. Sometimes the steps were flecked with patches of black, oozing slime.

Claudia tried not to let things bother here, but her hands were soon coated with a combination of everything she touched. "I have to wash my hands," she said.

"We will get out of here, Claudia," said Frank. "Be strong."

"I'm just so miserable. Got gook all over me and I stink. I'd give anything to be away from here safe and clean."

The stairs never seemed to end, one flight after another until she was a sweating, stumbling wreck.

"Two more flights, Claudia," said Frank, "come on you can do it."

He's lying, trying to motivate me. Or Peter.

Peter looked miserable too, but he must have been saving his breath. He wasn't any steadier on his feet than her, and was leaning heavily on the rail as they descended.

Frank, on the other hand, other than being dirty, still seemed fresh and alert. *What is with that guy---He's like a machine.*

"I'm ok Frank, let's go."

Frank started back down, and picked up his pace a bit. "Come on, we really are near the end."

Claudia and Peter followed him down the rest of the way.

"Smells like the sea," said Peter, "and something else."

At the bottom, the stair opened out past two long rotted doors into a cavernous room. A scummy-looking green slime mold floated on top of four or five inches of the seawater that covered the floor. Here and there, the old floor tiles were still visible. Some sunlight came through a line of broken windows lining two sides of the room. *Must have been some kind of waiting room.* Couches, easy chairs and tables rose from the water covered with a thin sheaf of the green scum.

The water closed around their ankles.

Thank God my boots are insulated.

Frank walked across the room, sending a trail of ripples through the water. He stopped by one of the windows and looked out. "We need to keep moving," he said, while poking out a shard of glass from the window frame. He then stepped over the sill and outside.

Claudia hurried over and followed him, with Peter right behind her. All three of them stood on a sidewalk next to the over-turned rusting hulk of a ground bus. A layer of mud has built up against the underside of the bus. A dozen small crabs darted toward holes and disappeared as she stopped near them.

The smell of the sea was even stronger outside. She could hear a seagull's lonely cry echoing off the walls of the ruins around her. Each building still standing was surrounded by water, probably only knee to waist deep, but the streets were covered.

"Still know where we are going, Frank?" asked Peter. His rifle was now held across both shoulders with his hands bracing it at either end.

Is he ever serious about anything?

"This way," Frank said. "I'll go first. You follow behind Claudia, ok Peter?"

"Sure thing."

Frank stepped off the curb, cautiously, found his footing and waded into waist deep water. Without thinking, Claudia forced herself to follow and felt cold water flow over the top of her boots and enter her suit through various rips and tears. The shock of it made her gasp, but it soon felt almost refreshing versus the heat and mugginess in the air.

Wonder how filthy this water is? Clean or polluted? Worst

part is not being able to see anything lower than mid thigh. She held the rifle ready, and felt the tension ratcheting her pulse rate up while waiting for something to burst from the water and eat her.

They tried to stick to the sidewalks.

Frank couldn't lead them straight to their destination. Too much rubble. Whole blocks of the city had been pulverized, and many of them were impassable due to deep water. At last, though, they stood on a patch of dry ground and were standing in the shade of some immense oak trees. Just in front of them was a long sward of waist-high grass.

A block or so away were a line of warehouses, and three starships: One shuttle; one atmospheric tug; and one that looked like an interstellar yacht.

In front of it all was a chain link fence. Outside of the fence, close to a score or more figures were milling about: Shabbily dressed, ragged looking people. Several had a hold of the fence and were shaking it. Some of the people were moaning loudly.

"This can't be good. Is that where you are taking us, Frank?" asked Peter.

Frank turned toward them with a bland expression. "Yes. Closest transport off planet. That yacht would be perfect. All the speed we need to escape anything short of a sunspot storm."

"Does sound good," Claudia heard herself say. Just thinking of the luxuries that might be aboard such a vessel was tantalizing.

"Those buildings," Frank said with a nod toward the warehouses, " are one of their cloning facilities. They clone people, and then infest them with a controlling parasite, or a sentient personality fragment of a long dead alien, if you will. These creatures have been at war with humanity before. One of our scout ships just had the misfortune of finding one of their home worlds is all."

"You do know a lot about them, now, don't you? Peter asked.

"Enough to horrify me, yes."

Claudia stepped forward next to Frank, "Let's get this over with. I just want to get out of here."

"Ok Claudia, here's what I want you to do. Clear out any of the creatures that are in your way and make straight for the gate."

Claudia held up a hand, "How do we know those people aren't friendly?"

"Trust me, they aren't. Just listen! Blast open the gate if you have to, but head straight for yacht and get in. Peter and I will be right behind you taking out the rest and watching for guards. Got it?"

Both she and Peter nodded, then all of them broke into a jog.

Frank

Any hesitation is probably going to be fatal.

He could see the doubt on both of their faces when he asked them to trust him. *How to explain quickly, though?* Once Dr. Gallows knew of their escape, the pursuit would be immediate and deadly.

As they drew closer, the stench of rot wafted to them on the breeze, then the detail of terrible, mortal wounds became obvious. These people couldn't be alive, but they were! The creatures weren't aware of them until they were scant yards away. In fact, Claudia managed to dodge two and get right up to those around the gate before they could react. She fired repeatedly into them from behind, tossing bodies and limbs in a long, near continuous explosion.

For a moment, nothing stood between her and the gate.

Frank fired a burst from the rifle that sent three of them spinning, one losing an arm and another losing both legs. The third one was caught beneath the falling bodies of the first two. He spun to his right, snapping off two shots. One bolt hit a middle-aged re-animated guy in the forehead and the other pinned a woman to a tree. *Must reach Claudia!* Even as he had that thought, out of the corner of his eye, he saw Peter go down, falling over backwards in the tall grass beneath another woman. Everything seemed to slow as he tried to process and decide what to do. Claudia had her back against the gate and was firing quick as she could as a ring of the creatures closed in.

Time ran out, as he turned toward the place Peter fell.

Peter screamed, long and loud. The woman was chewing on his arm! Blood fountained onto the woman and sprayed the grass. *Too late, too late!*

Frank changed course, hoping to save Claudia at least. He saw with relief that the creatures around her were all down and she was busy shooting the lock off the fence. At the last moment, he turned back toward Peter, barely stopping in time to avoid crashing into the woman.

She snarled up at him, as if to warn him off, as he raised the rifle high and slammed the butt down into her face. The horrible visage collapsed, crushed beneath the blow. Two more strikes put her down for good. Peter's features were gray, and his body prone. *No time to think. Must hurry!* He scooped the other man up, and slung him over his shoulder.

The gate was open. Claudia ran across a stretch of bleached white concrete toward the yacht.

Frank followed, trailed by the remaining creatures.

<u>Peter</u>

He awoke laying his back on the warm concrete. His first instinct was to look at his injury, but he quickly discovered that someone had wrapped the wound and put his arm in a sling. He didn't really want to see what the woman's teeth did to him anyway.

The oddest sensation came from his wounded left arm. The pain of having his flesh ripped away was being replaced by a wave of terrible itching working its way through the veins of his ravaged arm and up into his shoulder.

He sat up, unable to stay still, and found himself on the floor of what must be one of the warehouse buildings. *But why? Why aren't we in the ship getting the hell out of here?*

"Oh God," he heard Claudia say, "you look terrible Peter!"

He tried to muster a grin, "Well thanks a lot. Something's in me. I can feel it."

Frank stood nearby looking at him. He didn't say anything, but Peter knew it was bad.

"Why aren't we in the ship?"

Claudia answered, "It has a magnetic lock. All three ships are held in place by a magnetic field built into the landing pads. We have to find the control room to shut it off."

"Well, we better go then," he said and gritted his teeth, using his good arm to lever himself to his feet. He looked around and realized he must have dropped his rifle. The pistol was still there, though. He slipped it from the holster and undid the safety.

Frank nodded, seeing that he was ready, and led the way

deeper into the building. The front entry, where they were, was little more than a room with some boxes shoved against the wall and another door. Frank crossed over to the other door with his rifle at hip level. The hum of machinery was audible through the door, now that they were close.

The other man opened the door and slipped through. Claudia motioned for him to follow. He wanted to argue, but knew he was a liability now. He'd have to defer to the other two or risk getting them all killed. He followed as quick as he could, and entered a long, wide hallway lined with at least two or three doors, each spaced about thirty feet apart. He joined Frank at the first door and peered through its built-in glass window.

The room held two rows of vertically mounted tanks, each containing the shadowy shape of what he presumed was a human figure. He could make out a head, torso and shoulders in each one. Surrounding each tank were various machines and instruments. Here and there were a few gurneys, complete with tie-downs.

He didn't notice any attendants.

"Can't imagine any controls to the pad being there," said Claudia.

"No," replied Frank, "let's keep going."

The next door down was an airlock door. The window looked in on a chamber large enough for perhaps twenty people if they were friendly. On the opposite wall was another airlock door. "This doesn't look good either," said Peter. "We better hurry too, I can feel whatever it is getting close to my neck."

"You can actually feel something inside?" Claudia asked, going pale.

"An itching sensation that burns. Who knows what it is really doing to me inside."

Frank jogged ahead, and glanced in the last door, as they followed at a slower pace.

Bet I can't run now, even if I wanted to.

"This might be it!" Frank shouted, opening the door.

By the time Peter and Claudia caught up, Frank was inside, hunched over a console. Overhead were at least twenty monitors, each apparently showing a different view of the facility grounds.

With a grunt, Frank flipped three switches, and three LEDs changed from active to inactive. "Has to be it. Come on!" he said, and once again resumed leading the way.

Another door was at the end of the hall. Frank told Claudia to go ahead, while he helped Pete, as they all filed back outside.

"Just relax," Frank said, "Put your arm over my shoulder."

Peter did as was asked, and Frank lifted him into his arms like a bride. Frank wasn't a large man, and despite his build, the feat came across as a little too effortless.

"You augmented or something?" Peter asked.

"Something like that," Frank answered, nearly sprinting in his effort to catch up with Claudia. The door to the yacht was already open. Frank had to lower him to the ground so they could climb in, but that didn't slow them very much.

The engines whined as Claudia powered them up. Frank

pulled the door closed and Peter settled into a seat.

Peter closed his eyes, finding it hard to believe they were actually pulling this off. Only the onward migration of the itching kept a smile off his face, that and a molten, acidic lump that was rising in his throat. "Oh Lord," he murmured, "what is happening to me?"

El-ick

The *SCAR* dropped into Earth space first. Space distorted, rippling, and then suddenly its massive form was there where before there was nothing. The badly damaged *Maggot* and *Wound* appeared seconds later. Four other ships were already near Earth. Without even consulting the sensor reading, El-ick recognized one of them immediately as the *Rot*. It was the vessel of the high commander, Garok. The *Rot* was the most advanced battleship of the fleet though it was small in size compared to the massive dreadnought he commanded. The other three vessels consisted of *The Worm, The Grave*, and *The Entropy*. El-ick didn't have to wonder why most of the fleet's main firepower had been called back to Earth. He could guess easily enough. Garok surely expected the colonies of Man to make an attempt to move against the Earth if there was any chance they had heard of the *Hyperion's* return. Recovering its experimental drive tech alone would be worth the attempt, but when it combined with the fact that it carried living humans and all the data stored within its systems of the ship's long voyage into uncharted space, an attempt at reclaiming it became a certainty.

"Open a channel to the Rot," El-lick ordered his comm. Officer. Garok's flawless, pink face appeared on the screen in front of him. If El-ick himself looked almost human, Garok was the perfect picture of a living man his age. El-ick knew Garok was not only his superior in command of the whole of the dead's fleet, but the most powerful unliving being on Earth, answering only to the council of elders that comprised the heart of Earth Command itself.

An eerie and condescending smile stretched over Garok's full lips as saw El-ick through his own view screen. "Welcome home, El-ick. Glad you could join us. I have a feeling we will be needing the *SCAR's* sheer power. There was not time to assemble more of the fleet. We are all that stands between Earth and the human fleet which is reportedly on its way."

El-ick shook his head. "Garok, you know very well that even if ships were not present the humans couldn't breach the Earth's orbital grid with anything short of a miracle."

El-ick watched as a crew member of *The Rot* handed Garok a mug of steaming blood where he sat in his command chair then darted out of view. Garok sipped at the red liquid before he continued, unconcerned with making El-ick wait. "What you say is true of course but where is the sport in that? Meeting them here is much more. . . arousing."

"There's no need to risk the ships of the fleet in this confrontation," El-ick warned him.

"If I want your opinion, El-ick, I will ask for it," Garok growled. "How badly damaged is *The Maggot*? Can she stand with us?"

"No," El-ick lied. *The Maggot* was indeed hurt but not so much as to keep out of a fight if the need arose. Her crew had been laboring on in flight repairs to her since the moment her last engagement ended. "She needs to be docked. Her hull integrity was compromised. Another lucky shot could tear her apart."

"Fine," Garok waved dismissively. "Send her to one of the

space docks inside the Grid's protection."

"This fleet you say is coming, what do we know about it?" El-ick demanded.

Garok tapped some controls on the arm of his chair. "I'm sending over the intel now."

El-ick looked down at the information uploading to the *SCAR* and directed a copy of it directly the tactical screen on the arm of his own chair. His eyes grew wide as he read the data. "Good lord," he muttered. "Are you sure this correct?"

"Yes. The scout ship, *Cancer*, accidentally stumbled upon the human fleet in the sector where it was amassing. The *Cancer* was destroyed but not before relaying this data via a Leap Space burst."

"If this is correct, this is almost the entire fleet of *all* the colonies combined and even some of the new ships they were in the process of completing. This makes no sense. Have the humans lost their minds?"

"Did you really believe anyone who still breathed was capable of rational thought or logic?" Garok laughed. "They are far too emotional to think clearly on any level."

El-ick leaned forward in his chair. "I request permission to take *The Wound* and whatever other ships you can spare back to the colonies immediately."

Garok smiled. "Request denied."

El-ick boiled with anger on the inside but managed to kept it from showing on his face or at least he hoped he did. "The colonies have to be almost defenseless, sir. There will never be a better time to strike them than now. It is without question, with so much of their strength headed here to engage Earth, the *SCAR* alone could eradicate one of them. Give me a few ships and I will end this long war."

"Did you not hear me El-ick? Your request is denied. Now move the *SCAR* and the *Wound* into position with the rest of my ships so that we may face the humans together the moment they leap in."

"As you say sir," El-ick answered struggling not show his utter contempt for Garok. "Do it," he ordered his helmsman. The *SCAR's* massive, sub-Leap Space engines flamed and the enormous dreadnought moved to its place behind *The Rot* and the other ships under Garok's command.

Frank

"We've got two fighters on our tail, guys!" Claudia said over her shoulder while sitting in the pilot's chair. The take-off was perfect and the yacht climbed rapidly into the sky with little discomfort.

Peter lay within the crèche of the robodoc, this one a far more advanced version than that of the *Hyperion*. Frank looked up, "Do your best Claudia. I think I'm losing him. He's got a fever and the shakes!"

"It burns! Oh dear Lord it burns! Help me!" shouted Peter.

Frank put a hand through the permeable field that surrounded the crèche and on to Peter's forehead. He was burning up and his face was ashen. A tremor racked his body and then the machine's alarm sounded. Blood vessels broke in Peter's eyes, and his face went slack as he quit breathing.

At the same moment, Claudia cried out, as she started a series of evasive maneuvers. Several of the ship's system monitors beaconed in protest, adding to the cacophony.

A soft tone signaled an incoming message, "Attention the yacht *Drachma*, you are commanded to stop and prepare to be boarded."

"We're about to clear the atmosphere, Frank. Half a minute more and we can leave these fools behind."

Frank didn't know what to say. It wasn't exactly a good time to tell her that Peter was dead. The man's sightless, staring eyes were hard to take. He had to do something, so he reached out to close his eyelids. He pressed down on the now cooling flesh and felt movement! The shock of it paralyzed him for a moment. *He's dead!* The robodoc's readouts still supported this.

"Frank, they're shooting at us!" shouted Claudia.

A moment later, Frank watched as Peter grabbed his hand, jerked it toward his mouth and bit down! *Ah, the pain!* He tried to jerk his hand free, but Peter was using both hands now and his grip was incredible. Frank watched the skin and fatty tissue of his finger peel away from the bone. With his left hand he punched Peter and pulled his hand free, but not before another long strip of his flesh was stripped away. The pain shut down almost immediately, but the damage was done.

Oh God! He thought and stared, holding his hand up. The ferro-plasticized alloy composition of part of his hand and finger was completely exposed, with only shreds of flesh left hanging.

No hiding it now. Claudia would soon know what he was, and that he wasn't human, but he didn't have time to worry about that.

Frank searched frantically across the robodoc's control panel finally finding the lock-down button. He activated the field just as Peter was sitting up.

Claudia must have noticed something. She rushed across the cabin to his side. "What's happened? Oh no, look at him Frank! His mouth is all bloody!"

"Make sure he doesn't get loose!" Frank ordered Claudia as he stood up, riveted to the yacht's alarm beacons screaming for his attention. He hid his hand from view as he darted by her to the pilot seat. The *Drachma* had cleared the atmosphere leaving the two atmospheric fighters behind and helpless to follow them. Frank's relief became terror as he stared out of the Yacht's front window. "Oh God," he muttered. He hadn't worried about escaping through the Earth's defensive grid, it was only designed solely to face external threats, but he had never remotely imagined having to deal with what he now faced. A battle larger than any he'd ever seen raged among the stars.

A fleet of capital ships belonging to the dead squared off against what looked to be an entire human armada. He jerked the craft's controls hard to the right, barely avoiding a missile as it blew past them towards a black destroyer. His super human synaptic speed combined with the Yacht's mobility was all that had saved them from becoming space dust. Then he saw it directly in his flight path: A ship so large that it blocked the stars from view as he approached its underside. It stretched over two miles long and was half that in width. Its hull was midnight black streaked with silver and spotted with the scars of battle. It had to be a dreadnought class ship. Nothing else could be so huge. *Double the size of the old Julio Cesare they'd encountered not long ago. No sense comparing an old first rate heavy cruiser to the new dreadnoughts like this behemoth.* His heart sank as he realized it belonged to the dead.

A human fighter darted past him on his approach firing with all guns blazing into the thing. The fighter's fire didn't even penetrate the ship's armor and was no where near powerful enough to cause real damage. The best shots merely left dents on the black metal. The fighter continued straight on its course hurling itself into the massive ship's hull. Frank blinked as the fighter exploded leaving a hole where it had struck. Several bodies drifted into space from the opening. Drifted, he noticed. Apparently the big ship had no interior atmosphere or so little of one the rupture did not create the kind of venting into space it would have done with a human ship. The tiny figures bore arms and took pop shots at the nearest human fighters with small arms as they floated further into the darkness.

Space itself seemed to shake, though Frank knew that was a trick of the human part of his brain, as the dreadnought opened fire on the human fleet. He watched two human battleships destroyed instantly. The battle around them was growing more fierce and many of the dead ships had launched their own fighters now to engage the humans. *Drachma* was not designed for combat. It had no real armor. He needed to get them out of here before a rogue shot took them out. He looked at the enormous dreadnought and knew what he had to do. "Out of the frying pan, into the fire," he thought. If they wanted to survive, they were going to have to get aboard that thing.

He used the yacht's sensors to find one of the dreadnought's fighter bays and set a course for it. The big ship hadn't launched any fighters and he doubted it would. It seemed focused entirely on the humans' capital ships and taking them out as quickly as it could. He believed though, that if the technology the dead used was akin to the human tech he knew, he could safely get the yacht inside one of its bays. He punched up the yacht's speed and made his move.

Frank was not happy about what he was about to do. They would essentially be handing themselves over to the dead once more, but given that option or the near certain fate of a fiery death in the heart of the battle, he supposed surrendering at least left them alive with the chance they could escape again. He flew the yacht straight up and into one of the massive ship's hangars at full throttle, cutting back his speed at the last possible moment. The battle was intense and the sooner they got on board the better. He watched the hangar personnel scatter as the yacht made its way inside. The *Drachma* touched down on the metal of the hangar floor. "Frank!" he heard Claudia screaming from where he had left her with Peter.

Ka-Jhea

Ka-Jhea gritted her teeth, and used maximum thrust to power her *Hades*-class fighter up and out of the launch tube. On either side of the fighter's main body, the wings expanded their delta shape as she swept through two gears and switched to attack mode. Outside the cockpit there was no sound, no screams, no gunfire, or explosions---Just huge silent fireballs, streaking missiles and crisscrossing beams of energy.

None of that mattered. Too many distractions came from her thoughts anyway. She was monitoring both her own command channel and that of her enemy. Of course just watching one of her enemy's capitol ships explode and imagining the sound of ten thousand humans screaming as one provided her with a music that had a unique flavor of its own.

"Incisor Sixteen you have freedom of targets," said the voice of her commander from back on the command deck of the escort carrier *Pox*, or *Roma* as the humans once called her.

"Order acknowledged," she answered, and cut hard right on a course that would take her beneath *Pox's* massive underbelly. A swarm of enemy fighters and gunboats were even now conducting what appeared to be a suicide attack.

A list of potential targets immediately started to scroll down in a transparent window, seemingly floating in mid-air, just off center from her right eye. For the moment the closest targets were listed, rather than by the level of threat they presented. Her left hand trailed across the keyboard selecting a trio of gunboats that were making a run at *Pox's* starboard engine complex. They mounted an array of light defensive weaponry and two massive 300cm Hellbore cannon. Those cannon could gut most ships at close range and were designed for close-in attack.

"Going in, pursuing three *Hipper*-Class gunboats, Incisor Command! Incisor wing, cover my six!" Her two wingmen immediately pealed away and sought the escorting enemy fighters.

As her small fighter closed within a kilometer of the deadly, mite-sized but potent gunboats, she licked her lips, armed the missile array and settled her gun sight on the rear-most target. An acquisition signal beeped once, and she locked it down. One hundred uranium-tipped explosive rounds sped toward and through the closest gunboat and culminated in an out-of-proportion explosion that disintegrated all traces of the boat.

Next target acquired! Struggle to properly maintain target-lock status. She watched as the twin turrets spun in their mountings, seeking her ship out. Another burst from the her cannon raked the second boat and the resulting explosion flared brilliantly, leaving a pall of smoke and swirling fiery fragments in its place.

One more! She pulled her fighter into another tight turn in her attempt to stay behind the third gunboat. This last target pursued his own agenda despite the death of his comrades. Both of his Hellbores blasted away at the *Pox's* launching bays doing tremendous damage. The gunboat dodged right, and the cannons kept firing, trailing a line of destruction that must have reached stored fuel or ordinance in the landing bays. Several explosions shook *Pox's* frame and she realized that there would be no return for her there. The massive ship might even be in danger of a catastrophic explosion. There was nothing for it but to hunt down the enemy who did this.

The white hot exhaust of the gunboat drifted into her sights. She locked her weapons onto it and opened fire. The Hades' cannons blazed away. She watched with delight as the gunboats' engines ruptured and split, leaking fuel before it exploded into a ball of light and fire. The battle was drawing to close around her. The humans were turning tail. Their remaining large ships entering leap space and vanishing from the system. An alarm cried for her attention. Looking down she saw that her own fighter had sustained damage. The fighter needed to be docked now or she might end up adrift and be forced to suffer a long and intolerable wait for a rescue crew to pick her up. She laughed as she noticed the closest ship was the *SCAR*. Ka-Jhea had heard tales of the mighty ship and its captain wasn't a captain at all but rather an admiral who refused to leave active duty behind despite his rank. The man's name was a legend among the dead who served in the Earth fleet.

"El-ick," she muttered in a tone of respect. Ka-Jhea opened a channel to the *SCAR* and requested permission to come aboard. The *SCAR* was the only ship of the fleet which hadn't launched fighters during the battle. None the less her request was granted. Her fighter spun on a dime, curving in space and streaked towards the massive dreadnought. With any luck, she'd find a new home there and eventually meet this "El-ick" so many living and dead alike feared. Then she saw it. "What the Hell?" she thought as the yacht darted into the *SCAR's* docking bay. *What was a civilian vessel doing up here in the middle of a fraggin' space battle, much less going aboard a ship like the SCAR?*

El-ick

The wait was a short one. The human fleet leapt into the system less than an hour later. Apparently they had been in route behind the *SCAR* and her support destroyers. Huge areas of the void rippled and tore as the human vessels emerged into real space. El-ick counted over two dozen destroyers, all seven of the humans' known battleships, two fighter carriers, and even several small frigates. El-ick shook his head at the level of stupidity the living could sink too. The *Rot* led the deads' own battleships and *his* destroyer, The *Wound*, which Garok had assumed command of as part of the battle group, to meet them. The humans' weapons were already blazing. Nuclear missiles streaked across the void towards the dead fleet. Scores upon scores of single man fighter craft were launching in a mad dash to reach the dead ships before counter fighters could be deployed. In this, the humans knew they had the upper hand. The living were a tiny bit faster than even the best of the dead when it came to reflexive response times. It made them better pilots and they liked to capitalize on this little advantage whenever they could.

El-ick scowled and pondered his course of action. He wanted no part of this battle. It was a waste of resources and an unneeded risk. The Earth's defense grid could easily handle anything this rag-tag fleet of human vessels were able to throw at it. Yet he could not simply stand by and do not nothing while watching his brothers meet true death. To end the battle quickly became his goal. "Helmsman, take us right down the humans' throats, full speed. Fire at will!"

As the first wave of human fighters reached the dead fleet and began strafing runs   against the deads' battleships, the *SCAR* rocketed forward. It moved between the two fleets paying no heed to the small fighters swarming it. Tiny explosions danced up and down its sides as their weapons struck its hull. The *SCAR*'s railguns opened up first. Trails of projectiles cut their way through space, slicing two of the human battleships in half. Then the *SCAR* made its real move. Its near planet killer level of missile tubes spat death into the human ranks. One of the fighter carriers took over a dozen direct nukes and lit up like a fireball, taking a new wave of launching fighters with it. Three of the other human battleships also took hits but none severe enough to fully cripple them.

El-ick's eyes scanned the battle reports and sensor data being fed to the screen on his chair. So far only one dead ship had been lost.   The *Worm*, double teamed by two of the human ships, was caught between their volleys of fire and broke apart into pieces, as their cannons blazed away into it. El-ick held his fighters in reserve. He had no need to give the order for them to launch. It would take a miracle for the human fighter to do any real damage to a vessel the size of the *SCAR* and the other ships under Garok's command had already launched theirs. El-ick tapped into the comm traffic of the area and listened to the calm voices of the dead as they were atomized and the humans screaming as they met death. Countless tiny blossoms of flame bloomed and vanished in the darkness of space. As he predicted the deads' fighters were vanishing in triple the number that the humans' were. This battle belonged to the dead.

He would see to that. He ordered his gunners to direct their fire solely at the lead human battleships. Within seconds another exploded and another was crippled. He could hear the cries of "Fallback!" and "Retreat!" being shouted over and over on the human frequencies.

A second dead battleship left this plane of existence as a nuke struck its main engine and it went up like a grenade, spraying shrapnel into the ships around it. The human ships began to make the jump to leap space despite the small victory of seeing another dead vessel destroyed. El-ick wondered how much damage they would have inflicted on Garok and his fleet had the *SCAR* not been present.

El-ick causally nodded to Dirk to keep firing as long as they had targets. A stream of fire from one of the *SCAR's* railguns tracked a human frigate and blew it to shreds just as its engines were reaching leap speed. El-ick noticed the human vessels were so desperate to get away, they were leaving many of their fighters behind. It was very unlike them. "Dirk, concentrate the railguns on the fighters. I don't want a single human left alive out there."

"Yes sir!" Dirk barked back at him.

The humans had paid dearly for their foolish act. They had lost four of their remaining battleships, seven or more of their destroyers, all the frigates that they had brought into the Earth system, and only God knew how many fighters. Much of this was the *SCAR's* doing and he was sure the legend of his massive and mighty dreadnought would continue to grow among the human in the colonies. Some of his own crew joked that he was the lord of death. He could scarcely begin to imagine what the humans must think of him.

Frank

The shuttle came to a stop. Claudia was yelling and Peter was trying to get free of his restraints. Frank knew the dead outside the yacht would soon be forcing their way inside. "Claudia!" he shouted. "Forget about Peter and hide!" He figured Peter would be safe. He was infected with the dead virus now. Soon he would be one of the enemy. They would likely let him live and enter their society. Claudia however was in great danger. The initial boarders would come in guns blazing, no doubt believing the yacht was an assault shuttle. He would meet them and give them the fight they were looking for. When they were done with him, Claudia's chances of survival would be much higher if they found her whimpering somewhere and not making a stand against them.

He heard the noise of a charge detonating and the yacht shook violently. They were inside. He darted through the cargo hold. Peter growled at him as he passed, flinging saliva into the air like a mad dog. Frank saw the first two of the dead step through the blown airlock into the yacht. He rushed them head on. He hit the first one so hard, the impact flung the man back outside of the yacht and sent him skidding along the hangar floor.

The second attacker reached out for him to try to restrain him but Frank caught his arm and snapped it off. The man stared at him in shock as Frank's hands found the sides of his head and with a mighty twist tore it from the dead soldier's shoulders. Frank felt a jolt as a taser like dart embedded itself in his right arm. Thankfully, he was insulated against such an attack. Nothing short of a full out

EMP could shut him down that way. He emerged from the ship to face a semi-circle of six more of the dead. Some of them wore armor and others merely the work suits of engineers. Frank paused a fraction of a second, with the sadness of someone who knows they are about to cease to exist, then leapt from the yacht onto the closest of the dead. His fingers buried themselves in the chest of one of the engineers and with a heave, he ripped the man's rib cage apart and tossed him to lay crippled on the floor, trying to scoop his organs back inside of himself.

A soldier struck Frank in the jaw with the butt of his rifle. Frank's head rattled and his synthetic flesh tore along his cheek, exposing metal underneath. He caught the soldier's weapon and jerked it from his hands. He turned it on the others and shot two in the head before they knew what hit them. Frank was suddenly flung forward. Someone delivered a perfectly placed kick to his back which likely would have shattered a human's spine. He toppled face first to the metal of the floor and rolled to his feet. He came up facing a woman who wore the suit of a pilot. She was strikingly beautiful despite being dead. Her skin was a light shade of gray but not decayed and her body was tight with well developed and shaped muscle. She flicked long black hair from her face with a twitch of her head as she took a martial arts stance Frank was unfamiliar with and stood beckoning for him to make a move at her. The other dead had backed off seemingly content to watch what unfolded between the pilot and himself. He lunged at her swinging a hard right at her face. She ducked under it and came up with a jarring blow to his chin that left even him stunned. Following up with a kick to his torso, she put him on the floor again. Frank had to admit he was impressed. He started to get to his feet but found himself staring at the barrels of three rifles as the dead who had been watching closed in on him and took advantage of the chance the pilot had given them. Frank opened his mouth to tell them he surrendered but the thunder of their rifles never gave him the chance. His form bounced and vibrated as a slew of rounds blew holes in the flesh covering his true form and left dents in the metal underneath. The last thing Frank saw as the darkness took him was the female pilot standing nearby laughing.

Claudia

Frank had told her to hide. She could hear the sounds of battle raging outside of the yacht. She simply couldn't bring herself to follow his orders though. She stood watching Peter struggle against his bonds. She flinched every time pieces of his skin were ripped away but he didn't seem to notice the pain at all. "Oh Peter," she thought. "It's not fair. We finally make it home after all those years and the Earth is dead."

Peter leaned forward as far as he could and snarled at her with hungry eyes. His sudden move caused her to retreat a step. As she did, the noise of armored boots clanking on the yacht's floor caused her to turn around. Two men, she guessed though she really couldn't tell because of the full body combat suits they wore, entered the yacht and moved towards her.

"On the floor!" one of them ordered. Claudia had no choice but to comply. She raised her hands behind her head and sunk to her knees.

"I surrender!" she yelled at them. "My friend is infected. Will you help him?" she pleaded not knowing what else to do. The men laughed and one of them lifted a rifle in her direction. She opened her mouth to protest but the rifle cracked sending a dart flying into her chest. She looked down to see it protruding from her sternum as she was overcome by feeling a lightheadedness. She wobbled on her knees and collapsed sideways as her eyes closed themselves and sleep over took her.

El-ick

El-ick stood before the mirror in his ready room with anger seething through every molecular cell of his form. Garok had crossed the line this time. The pink faced bastard was actually filing court martial charges against him and the crew of the SCAR for not following direct orders during the battle with the human fleet. The man had sent him an encrypted message stating as much as soon as the battle had ended. "The fool!" El-ick raged and smashed his fist into the mirror, shattering it and sending shards of glass clattering to land at his feet. He looked at his hand and cursed himself for letting anger get the better of him. The skin grafts to repair the damage he'd just done were not going to be cheap by any means. He picked at the pieces of glass stuck in his flesh as he gritted his teeth. Like all the dead, except for the extremely powerful of the intelligent dead like Garok and the council members who could afford sensory implants directly in their brains, he felt no pain. His nerves had long rotted away into nothingness.

Had it not been for the actions of the *SCAR*, the dead would have lost a great deal more in the skirmish but Garok had a following and knew just the right ears into which to whisper his claims. He was going to lose command of the *SCAR*. It didn't matter that he was a legend among the fleet. His years of loyal service and long lists of victories would be forgotten in favor of the word of man who came to his position through bribery, murder, and cunning. El-ick understood Garok's line of thinking. The man wanted him gone simply because El-ick was the sole threat to his one day taking command of all of the Earth fleet and the world itself. He knew Garok likely had a similar plan with which he would eventually dispose of the council and become the emperor he so long wanted to be.

El-ick weighed his options carefully in his mind. He could stand trial. In fact, it was his duty to do so and hopefully prove what Garok's motives for bringing the charges against him truly were or he could go rogue and take the *SCAR* into deep space, leaving behind his world in order to keep his ship and perhaps one day return to see Garok face justice.

The military man in him wrestled with duty to the service and duty to the race of the dead itself. Garok could not be allowed take complete power. He would squander everything so many had perished to build since their race was born. El-ick nodded to himself and knew in that moment he would never surrender the SCAR without a fight. She was his and his alone. The ship gave his life purpose and meaning. El-lick looked over his shoulder as the door to his ready room opened and Captain Dirk entered.

"Sir, there's been an attempt to board the ship. I think you should come see what's happening in the hangar bay."

El-ick cocked an eyebrow at Dirk. He shook the last of the glass from his hand and said, "I am on my way."

El-ick took a moment to gather himself and then followed Dirk onto the bridge on his way to the lift down to the hangar bay. He didn't make to the lift. Crewman North, who sat the sensor station, became screaming. "We've got incoming!"

Both El-ick and Dirk were taken aback. "What the hell?" Dirk blurted. "I thought the last of the human fighters were destroyed."

El-ick raced to his command chair and called up the data on the approaching ships. There were six assault shuttles with a squad of fighters flying escort en route to the *SCAR*. He identified them instantly part of the the *ROT*'s contingent. "Garok," he said the name aloud like a curse word, hatred and anger dripping from his voice.

"What do we do sir?" North asked stating what every officer on the bridge must be thinking. "They're hailing us," the Com. Officer informed him. "They're demanding we surrender at once under the authority of fleet commander Garok. They want to board us and I quote sir, so that you can be properly relieved of command."

El-ick noticed Dirk cut his eyes towards him. The captain looked eager to see what his reaction would be. He knew that Dirk understood his philosophy, the importance of the lives of the dead men and women of the fleet. To him, they were not expendable as Earth Command would have him think of them.

"Take us into Leap Space now!" El-cik ordered. "Maximum thrust!" The stars rippled around the SCAR the huge ship blinked away, leaving the shuttles and fighters behind.

Ka-Jhea

Ka-Jhea watched as the human female was lead out of the yacht and taken away in custody by two armored soldiers. The robot lay in the hangar unmoving. Several more soldiers were in the process of cleaning up the mess from the fight and preparing to take it away as well. Most of the personnel in the hangar were still congratulating her on taking it down so easily. Engineers walked by patting her on the back and soldiers nodded at her with respect. It wasn't often a pilot was as well trained in hand to hand as she was.

"What is that thing?" one of the engineers, an older looking man who the years hadn't been kind to with skin that was literally peeling off his bones, asked her.

"It's a class X3 android. The kind humans used to use on extended space missions to keep an eye on the crew or to make sure there was someone there to get the vessel home if the crew fell to radiation storm, virus, or the like," she explained.

"Hmmph," the old man snorted, "I thought all those things were wiped out."

"Apparently not," Ka-Jhea smirked. "The bugger sure knew how to fight. I heard rumors among the fleet that the deep space exploration vessel the *Hyperion* had returned with its crew intact. I would bet this week's pay that thing came back with them."

"There's an infected human on the yacht too," the old man grinned. "Have you gone in there to see him yet?" Ka-Jhea shook her head in the negative. "I hear they're trying to decide whether to put him down or send him to the pens with the others ferals." Ka-

Jhea looked at the old man clearly confused.

"I thought admiral El-ick didn't keep ferals aboard the SCAR."

"He doesn't," the old man confirmed. "I meant shipping him over to one of the vessels that does keep the animals on board for use in ground combat. The *SCAR* doesn't do ground combat. It doesn't need to. If our ship shows up in orbit, you can bet the humans best be crappin' their pants and prayin' they got enough orbital defenses or ships to get us to go away. They know the *SCAR* can and will just kill them all from space. It's what this beautiful monster of a lady was built for," he finished waving a hand around at the walls of the *SCAR*'s hull.

Ka-Jhea watched him hurry away to help with the repairs on her fighter. She wandered through the area of the hangar bay looking for the deck officer. She needed to check in and make sure that he allowed her to sign on as part of the *SCAR*'s compliment. This was a chance that only came along once and she knew it. There was no way she was going back to another ship if she could somehow stay here and serve under El-ick. She longed to meet the man who had become such a legend. On this ship, she could truly make a difference in the war effort against the colonies under his command. Unlike Garok and many of those in Earth Command planet-side, El-ick wanted the war over and was often too vocal, in her opinion, about the need to bring peace back to the galaxy through any means necessary. While she was aware he was in favor of wiping out the humans to end their threat, she wondered just how far he would go to see the dead under his command stop meeting the true death. She set herself up to be disappointed with her high, perhaps even unrealistic expectations of the man, but she couldn't help it. Ka-Jhea spotted the deck officer standing in a group of engineers giving reports on the battle damage the *SCAR* had taken and started on a path across the bay towards him.

Ron

Captain Ron Davis watched the two suns of the Alpha Centauri system as he sat at his post atop the hill above the spaceport. Alpha Centauri Prime was home to over seven million living souls and the heart of the remnants of human civilization. The city of New Charlotte was a gleaming testament to what mankind was capable of at its best. The high spires of staggeringly tall apartment and government buildings reached into the blue sky. Air cars whined through the spaces between them as the day went on as normal. "And why shouldn't it?" Ron wondered to himself. He had heard the news of the failure of the fleet to penetrate the Earth's defenses but then did anyone really think they had a shot at doing so? The losses to the fleet were heavy and that was the scary part. A lot of folks in the city were in a panic over it. If the dead came calling now, it was unlikely any of the colonies would be able to hold its own without the full force of the fleet to help in protecting them. People were terrified the dead would be coming and soon for surely the rotting monsters could clearly see how vulnerable they were until more ships were built. Their dreams were full of howling dead things running across the plains of Alpha Centurai Prime towards the great city of New Charlotte with blood smeared mouths and hungry eyes in numbers far too great to be stopped.

Ron lit up a cigarette and puffed on it wiping at the sweat on his forehead with the back of his hand. The suns were hot today. He exhaled blowing rings of smoke up at the cloudless sky. It was a nasty habit and one that was for the most part long dead. He had to grow his own tobacco just to be able to keep doing it. He was well aware of the social stigma that was attached to the habit but his rank as an officer in the planet's infantry spared him from being outcast and looked down upon like a civilian smoker would have been.

Private Chad Morris came sauntering up the hill to the lookout post where he sat. He smiled at the private, glad to see relief arrive. His shift had stretched over twelve hours as it was and he needed a drink. The private saluted, and he saluted back as soon as he got to his feet. He collected his rifle from where it sat propped beside him. Watches and outposts like this one were demanded by the people of the city. If the dead leaped into the sector unnoticed and shot "feral" pods onto the planet's surface, it would be up to men like him and those under his command to notice their approach and hold the dead off from the city long enough for the proper defenses to be laid or the populace to escape.

The ferals were the dead's shock troops. They had no other purpose. When the disease or whatever it was which reanimated the dead and gave them life it left them in a state of insanity much like an animal driven mad from hunger. It took time for their bodies to adjust to their new state of unlife and develop into the thinking dead who were the real enemy. The ferals were expendable infantry and nothing more until they survived long enough to become a true member of dead society. Ron had fought ferals before long ago when the dead first began to walk and overran the Earth. He remembered the way the things stank and their gangrenous green skin peeling from their face at it rotted. The things were near impossible to stop without a head shot. Anything less still left them dangerous even if they were in pieces. He'd witnessed a soldier once step too close to a head that had been blown off its body, but without destroying its brain, and saw the man put his foot just close enough to the thing's yellow teeth for it to roll over and bit him above the area covered by the thick leather of his combat boots. Their howls haunted him in his dreams to this day.

"Yep, it was definitely time for a drink," he thought. Chad entered the small, roofless bunker. "Thanks," Ron said. "Make sure you stay alert. The big wigs are keeping a close eye on because the trouble in space. Got it?"

"Yes, sir," Chad replied as Ron left and headed out onto the sand. Ron made his way to the base of the dune where military grade, one person, ground based APCs waited. He hit a button on his remote and the canopy of the one that belonged to him opened as he approached. Ron slid into the seat and the vehicle sealed its self, establishing its own internal atmosphere. Cranking up the "AC" and his music, Ron kicked the APC into gear as an old Earth band called AC/DC rocked through the speakers. A cloud of sand flew into the air as the APC streaked towards the gleaming city of New Charlotte below.

Claudia

Claudia awoke screaming. Her yells echoed off the metal walls of the cell she lay in. The room was empty. There was no bed, toilet, or anything. Just herself and the electro-field that kept her locked inside it. Her head ached like someone had smashed in her skull with a sledge hammer. Slowly and gently, she used her arms to push herself up and make it to an upright position. It took her a moment longer to gather her strength enough to get to her feet. Finally, she rose and made her way to the bars. It was very cold and the air felt thin. It was clear the dead had increased the almost nonexistent atmosphere of their ship in an attempt to better accommodate her and keep her alive. Too bad the bastards can't feel well enough to know when it's freezing, she thought as the cold sank deeper into her bones and she rubbed at her arms as she hugged herself.

"Claudia?" a strangely familiar voice asked from the cell across the hall. She strained her eyes but couldn't quite make out the shape of the man who spoke to her. The voice sounded a lot like Frank but it was off somehow. There was something different about it. It had almost a sort of metallic sound to it.

"Frank?" she asked. "Is that you?" She saw movement in the darkness of the cell as the figure got up and came closer to the cell's bars.

"Yes, it's me Claudia," he answered, and stepped into a bar of light.

She gave a little gasp. *Why am I so surprised? Not like I*

didn't know androids existed.

"So many secrets Frank, I don't really know you at all, do I?"

"I guess not."

Just looking at him unnerved her. Nothing of the man she knew remained. *Nothing of a man, either*, she thought with a measure of sadness and disgust. *Somehow, I knew. Must've been why I picked Peter. I knew. He's a thing. Not alive at all. If I close my eyes, all of this can be a nightmare. Frank can still be a living, breathing person, and Peter won't be dead.*

"I am distressing you. Try to think of me solely as a guardian, and maybe it will be easier. We were never meant to be more than acquaintances."

"Yes, Frank, I see that now, but it is too much seeing you like this."

"I understand, Claudia. I tried so hard…"

"I know Frank," she said, and forced herself to really look at him.

His true form, if you could call it that, was made of a pale ferro-plasticized alloy known for its strength and malleability. Close to indestructible. His eyes were a striking color of jade, and the nose little more than a stub. No ears that she could see, no hair, just the pale skin with its underlying, intricate tracery of veins, strands of muscle and tendon flowing through his body.

"What was left of me wasn't salvageable. The virus was loose in my flesh. Its taint could not reach my core, but I was forced to shed my shell due to the amount of damage they had inflicted on it. The worst part is that now they know what I am. The element of surprise is lost. There will be no escape for us this time."

"What about Peter? Did you-"

"I don't know what happened to him."

"Then, he may still be alive?"

"I hope not Claudia. Hopefully he's gone. From what I understand of the dead, based on the information I scanned from their computer systems back on Earth, they go through a period of being feral, hunger driven monsters at first. This period can last days or even many months depending upon the person. The dead look down on these feral monsters and have little regard for their lives, if you can call them that. Assuming Peter lives through the feral period it is likely he will regain his intellect but not necessarily any recollection of who he was when he was alive. Some of the dead do and others do not. Regardless, he will be like a child, learning and growing as his mind slowly turns on once more and his powers of reasoning increase."

"Where do you think they took him?"

"Most of these ferals are kept in pins or cages and used as shock troops for the dead's navy and armed forces. However, given our proximity to Earth, it is possible that they have shuttled him back to the planet to let him develop into one of the thinking dead in the hopes that he will retain his memories and be able to share his knowledge of the *Hyperion*, its mission, and drive tech with them."

<u>El-ick</u>

Dirk stood beside El-ick in the lift as it shot down towards the ship's brig where the unexpected intruders were locked away inside the ship's detention cells. "Garok isn't just going to let us go sir." "Stop," El-ick said the ship's AI ordering the lift to come to a halt in its transit. He turned to Dirk. "Garok is and always has been a fool. The man thinks of nothing but himself and personal gain."

"You should have made a move against him before now," Dirk stated.

"Politics are not my concern. I have no desire for power beyond that I need to help protect our world and our race but I will not stand idly by anymore and let Garok throw away all we have worked for since our race was born."

"Garok has more of an upper hand than ever now sir. Your inaction and faith in our people to deal with him on their own has left us in a much weaker position. You did disobey his orders during the skirmish with the humans. The *SCAR* was supposed to hold back while his ships engaged them."

"You know as well as I do how many of us I saved from the true death by disobeying Garok's idiot orders!"

"Indeed sir, I do. I agree wholeheartedly with your actions. I just do not believe that the council shall see it that way. Perhaps in the early days, before we got the clone machines online and were able to propagate our species, yes, but now, they will not care how many you spared. The navy, like the ferals, are expendable as long as Earth herself stays safe. They will back Garok's claims and he will come for us with everything he can muster."

"The *SCAR*..."

"The *SCAR* is an awesomely powerful ship sir but it is not indestructible."

"Dirk," El-ick warned, "do not talk down to me as I were Garok. I know full well the danger we face. I also know we can not run forever. I will devise a way to deal with Garok and get us out of current mess. I assure you. Now, I believe we have prisoners to deal with, yes?" El-ick changed the tone of his voice and spoke to the lift. "Resume." he ordered and their journey to the brig began again.   As the lift doors opened and the pair stepped out into the security level, Dirk took the risk of angering El-ick further.

"May I at least ask where we're headed sir?"

"Alpha Centuri," El-ick answered with a wide grin as Dirk stared at him in total shock.

Frank

Frank sat on his the single bunk in his cell. He did not truly need to rest in the human sense, it was just more comfortable for him at the moment. Claudia had withdrawn into herself. Whether it was from the loss of Peter or the shock of his own revelation, he couldn't say. She lay on the bunk of her own cell, curled up into a ball, underneath the bunk's blanket. The door to the cell block they were on slid open and he saw to the two armored guards outside standing at attention as two other men entered and approached him. Both were of course dead but one of them looked passably human. There were no obvious signs of decay on his face and his movements were as graceful as a cat's. He was clearly the ranking officer. The man beside him followed his lead and though younger in general appearance was certainly not in as good of shape. His skin was a sickly, pale gray and his eyes were red looking to be filled with dried blood. The one Frank guessed was in charge walked straight up to his cell and stood in front of him. Frank thought about grabbing the man through the bars and loosing his anger on him or perhaps using him as means to freedom if he could get the proper hold upon on. He dismissed the idea quickly though. There was something in the way the man looked at him that told Frank he not only knew what Frank was thinking but was more than prepared for anything Frank might try.

"My name is Admiral El-ick Jordan. You are currently aboard my ship, the *SCAR*. I need to know who you are and why you came aboard my ship. I will ask only once."

"I am a class X3 android designed to. . ."

"I know what you are," El-ick cut him off. "I want to know who you are."

"My name is Frank," he started again. "I am from the deep space exploration vessel called The *Hyperion*. We were on a five year mission to explore beyond the boundaries of known space. We returned home to find your race in control of the Earth and were captured. I managed to free myself and two of those under my protection. Using a stolen yacht, we left the Earth to find ourselves in the middle of the conflict in between your forces and those I presume of the human colonies. I saw no choice but to seek shelter from the battle and your ship was the best option available to me at the time. We boarded you to surrender rather than face certain death in space."

"I see," El-ick said. "One of those under your care is infected. For the time being, I am told that my security personal have him locked in a cell such as yours for his own protection. It appears his reaction to the virus is. . . abnormal. However, I confess, it has been so long since a real human has undergone the change where we could observe it, who can say with certainty what affect is has on a human not grown in a vat?"

Frank noticed Claudia had set up on her bunk. She sat watching the conversation he was having with the dead men but had not joined it.

"So Peter's alive?"

El-ick laughed. "As much as I am."

"Can we see him?" Claudia asked. Frank watched as El-ick spun on her, acknowledging her existence for the first time since entering the cell block.

"Trust me, you would not wish to. He is feral and dangerous. Perhaps, as time progresses, you might be allowed to see him assuming you are still alive yourself."

Frank moved next to the bars of his cell, drawing as close to El-ick as he could without appearing threatening.

"What do you want from us?"

El-ick titled his head as if surprised by the android's question.

"Clearly, you want something or we would be dead already," Frank added.

"The X3 series was well built I see. You are correct. I do need something from you. We are on our way to the heart of the remaining worlds of the human race, a world called Centuri Prime. Due to circumstances beyond my control, I find myself in need of, what do you humans call it, asylum?"

"And how are we to help with that?" Frank asked. "I have not seen a human outside of the *Hyperion's* crew in five years. We barely know anything about your war and the state of the galaxy. I have never even set foot upon Centuri Prime."

"True but I imagine they would take my request much more seriously and with luck even believe it if you and your human companion vouched for my ship and my crew."

"Why would we do that?" Claudia snapped. "You're all monsters, rotting sacks of soulless flesh that should be sent back to

Hell screaming."

"You're still breathing are you not?" El-ick moved to stand outside her cell. "I offer you freedom for yourself and the android if you help me. Besides, if you do not help, not even the *SCAR* can tackle the entire remnants of the human battle fleet alone. You will die in the cold, dark void of space along, with myself and my crew, as the humans scramble everything they have left to destroy us and this ship."

"If we help you, what happens to Peter?" Claudia demanded.

"I don't care. You may take him with you if you like though I highly doubt your kind will allow him to continue to exist. The danger of the virus getting loose in their cities would be too great."

"We'll help you," Frank said. He shot Claudia a look which told her to be silent. "We accept the terms of our freedom and Peter's in trade."

"Wonderful," El-ick smiled. "We should be arriving at Alpha Centuri Prime within the next few hours. I will have you brought to the bridge shortly before then so we plan how to approach the humans there together to best ensure survival for us all."

With that, El-ick and the lesser officer left them alone them in their cells. Frank watched Claudia closely. He could see the thing humans called hope returning to her eyes and he confessed to himself that the odds of them making it had greatly increased as well.

Peter

Peter woke hanging in a suspension web. The web was designed to keep him from damaging himself while at the same time keeping him held tightly in its restraining grip. There were no words capable of describing his pain. His thoughts were slow and cloudy. He struggled to remember who he was and what was happening to him. Peter's bloodshot eyes made their way around the room taking in the empty, black space. The room was dark and he was alone. A fresh wave of hunger hit him and he tried to scream at the pain but all that came out was an animal like howl. Flashes of memory sparked in his head. His name was Peter. Once long ago, it seemed, he had been a man. What he was now, he didn't know? Was this his home? No, he'd been trying to escape, get free of something beyond the bonds which held him but he didn't know what. He recalled a woman. He could see her clearly in his memories where so many other things were hazy or merely gone. Her name was . . . Claudia. Yes, that was it, Claudia, and she needed him. He struggled and squirmed trying to twist free. He gnashed at the web with his teeth. Peter looked up snarling as the door to his cell opened and a man entered. The man wore black combat armor but no helmet. His face was a mess of rotted flesh and wounds that would never heal. Peter watched as the man looked him over. Finally the man spoke in a cold, hollow voice. "Do you know your name?"

Peter strained to speak. "P-P-. . .et. .er."

"Impressive," the man commented. "It takes most ferals months to even understand what's being said to them."

Peter relaxed in the suspension web, hanging limply in its embrace.

"Well, Peter, you are aboard a ship called the *SCAR*. My name is Reaper. I am in charge of the *SCAR* marine unit. I'll give you a choice, if you want, I will draw my sidearm right now and send you on to the next life or you can join my men and learn how to be a person again, not just an animal ruled by the hunger you're feeling. Which do you want?"

"L. . . e. . .arn," Peter managed to get out the word though it took all his will to do so.

"Good," Reaper smiled. "I will give your mind a bit more time to finish waking up then I'll return so we can start your training." Reaper spun about and marched out of the room leaving Peter alone in the darkness once more.

Ron

Ron's R&R was cut short. He had no sooner gotten a comfortable seat at the bar and his hands on an ice cold beer when New Charlotte's defense sirens went wild, sending high pitched wails across the city at the same time as his personal comlink went off. Bitterly he placed his beer on the counter in front of him and flipped the link open. A tiny image of General Ackerman scowling at him from the link's screen. "Captain, why aren't you at your post?"

"On my way there now sir! What's going on?"

Ron listened to a brief and panicked explanation of what was happening in space, signed off, and dashed for his vehicle. Chad was still on watch when arrived at the outer bunker. Chad knew something was up. He too had heard the alarms it seemed. "Sir?" he asked as Ron stood checking the clip of his rifle.

"It's the *SCAR*," Ron informed. "Long range scanners say she's in Leap Space on her way here."

Chad went pale. They both knew there were only two ships currently in orbit around the Centuri Prime and one of those was undergoing massive repairs from the failed attack on Earth.

"I thought. . ." Chad started but Ron cut him off mid-sentence.

"Yes, Private, *The SCAR*. The one and only dreadnought in existence okay?"

"My God. . ." Chad muttered. "Why are they even bothering to scramble us then? The *SCAR* has never used a ground attack. It's just going to sit up there and pound us all to Hell."

"Because, Private, we're grunts and it's our fate to die out here alone. It's our job."

El-ick

El-ick sat in his command chair as the *SCAR* entered normal space and its standard thrusters kicked in. The massive dreadnought was fifteen minutes away from reaching orbit around Centuri Prime. He watched on the ship's view screen as a single human battleship moved to intercept them. It was hard not to laugh as he wondered what the poor, living captain of it must be thinking in this moment. He did not envy the man.

"Open a channel to that ship," El-ick ordered. "I want a chance to talk to them before we're forced to blow them out of the stars."

The face a man in fifties with short cropped gray hair and blue eyes appeared before El-ick. "This is Captain Blane of the Battleship *Griffin*. I order you to leave this space or we will be forced to engage you."

Good, El-ick smiled inwardly. The man did indeed know he had no hope against the *SCAR* even with Centuri Prime's orbital defense grid to back him up. The captain was desperate enough to talk and that was exactly what he wanted. "This is Admiral El-ick, in command of the Earth ship, *SCAR*. I suggest that you power down your weapons unless you really want to see what my ship is capable of. I've come seeking asylum. I and my crew only wish to be granted sanctuary."

Blane was stunned to silence. El-ick could see the utter shock in his eyes. Never before had a dead vessel requested human aid and the *SCAR* was far from an ordinary dead ship. She was a legend.

"Say again?" the captain asked.

El-ick leaned forward, closer to the screen. "I request sanctuary and refuge in human space. I am prepared to offer to add my ship to the defense of your world should the need arise."

The captain of the human ship clearly thought he was lying but there was hope, the hope of a man who seconds ago faced certain death and was suddenly given a chance to live, evident in his features. "How do I know this isn't a trick?"

El-ick motioned for Claudia to be brought forward into view of the screen. "This is Yeoman Claudia Coyne from the old Earth ship, the *Hyperion*, which as you know recently returned to Earth. She will attest to the sincerity of my claim."

"He speaks the truth, Captain Blane. I am one of three, er, I mean two survivors from *Hyperion*."

The captain looked at something off-screen. "Yeoman Coyne? We do show you in the crew's complement for the *Hyperion*, and your voice matches your record. How did you end up aboard the *SCAR*?"

"Upon our return home, the Hyperion was taken from us by force and myself, along with the entire crew, were captured. We were taken to Earth to be *processed.* Two of us managed to escape thanks to the efforts of the X3 android assigned to our ship. However, as we fled in a stolen ship, we found ourselves caught in the middle of your attack on Earth. Were it not for admiral El-ick, we'd be dead. I spoken with him at great length," El-ick watched as she spoke the well rehearsed lies he'd scripted for her, "and believe he speaks the truth."

The captain looked as if he had no idea to respond to the unimaginable events unfolding before him. "I will need to consult with the president of the Human Republic. In the meantime, hold your current position and do not approach the planet or you will be fired upon," with that he signed off and the *SCAR's* view screen reverted to an image of his ship which held its own position between the *SCAR* and the world of Centuri Prime.

"You did well," El-ick said to Claudia. "If he grants my ship sanctuary, you will soon be free and among your own people once more."

Claudia said nothing. El-ick motioned for the guard who had accompanied her to the bridge to lead her back to her cell. "Thank you," El-ick offered despite Claudia's coldness. The woman was rather fetching and he respected her strength in such dire circumstances as those she'd faced on Earth and aboard his ship.

As soon as she left the bridge, El-ick waved for Dirk to approach him. "The Hyperion, is it still in orbit around Earth?"

Dirk nodded. "It was when we left the system. I imagine it's still undergoing study at the space dock it was assigned to upon arrival."

El-ick's lips parted in a smile. "Dirk, I want you to prepare an assault team. We have three shuttles outfitted with the new smaller Leap drives. Go back there and bring me that ship."

Dirk stared at El-ick. "Sir?"

"You heard me captain," El-ick ordered more firmly. "I want it here by tomorrow. Take as many marines as you feel you need."

Reaper

Reaper stood in the training area, yelling at the men who were sparring to keep their hand to hand skills sharp as he pushed them on. Reaper would've blinked in surprise as the captain entered but his eyes lids had been gone for years, burnt off by a nearly too close of a call with a human grenade during the last days of the conflict for the control of the Earth. He snapped to attention as Dirk approached him.

"At ease commander," Dirk ordered. Reaper relaxed a by a tiny fraction.

"To what do I owe the pleasure of this visit?" he asked.

"I need you and two dozen of your best. The Admiral has deemed it fit for us to return to Earth via shuttle and steal the old Earth ship the humans came home in."

Reaper whistled. "He does like impossible tasks doesn't he? That ship will be guarded heavily. If I understand correctly, Earth Command desperately wants the proto-type drive it was launched with all those years ago. I am sure they've already assigned several science and engineering details to take a look at it and how it functions aboard the ship. In fact, there's no guarantee that they haven't already gutted that ship sir and took the drive back to Earth to study. She's been home a while now. What does he expect us to do if we get there and take the thing only to be stuck without no way to leap out of the system after we have her?"

Dirk shrugged. "He's El-ick. I imagine he expects us to perform a miracle."

Reaper grunted. "I'll get my team together. How long do we have?"

"I will be leading this mission personally," Dirk informed him, "I want you and your men waiting in the *SCAR's* port hangar bay in less than an hour."

The three shuttles dropped out of Leap Space close enough to be inside the atmosphere of the Earth's moon if it had one. Twin missiles streaked from each shuttle targeting the small outpost on the surface. The outpost erupted into a ball of fire and flying shrapnel. Reaper let out a cry of triumph where he stood above Dirk in the pilot's compartment. He noticed Dirk even allowed himself a grin.

"W e're all clear," Dirk said.

Reaper nodded, "Phase one, complete." The outpost was the only monitoring on the dark side of the moon and they were now totally invisible to the Earth unless they had the bad luck of an actual warship passing by them during their stay and they didn't plan to stay long. Just long enough to punch in a new set of coordinates and make the final jump into the space dock which held the *Hyperion* its self.

"This plan is crazy," Dirk commented.

Reaper laughed, "It's your plan sir."

"I know, why do you think I am so scared?" Dirk joked back trying to break the tension. "Locking coordinates now," Dirk's fingers flew over the shuttle's controls.

The plan was to Leap into the docking station literally. The combat shuttles' heavy armor would protect them, they hoped, while the disturbances hit the dock like a series of nukes. Reaper figured Dirk thought this would leave them in a state of shock while also inflicting heavy losses on the station's personal. Their team would ditch the shuttles, which would be useless and barely hanging together after such a stunt, and head directly for the *Hyperion*, shooting anything in their path that so much as moved. Once aboard, they'd fire up the old ship's engines and get the hell out before the Earth Command troops even knew what was happening. Reaper would've held his breath as Dirk finished his programming and hit the leap drive but he hadn't bothered to take one. The shuttles blinked out of normal space once more.

This time when the shuttles dropped out, Reaper was thrown all the way back through the ship to bounce off the rear wall. His heavy armor clanged as metal struck metal and he landed face first on the floor. He pushed himself up, spitting teeth.

"Damn it!" Reaper cursed.

The shuttle's aft door opened behind him as he leapt to his feet and followed Dirk and his men out. They were all lucky to still be existing. The shuttle looked like a mangled dog toy. The area inside of the dock around it, looked even worse. Patches of stars could be seen through holes in the station's walls and truly dead Earth personal floated in their path, twisted and broken bodies careening this way and that in the now zero G environment. If the station had contained a real atmosphere like the ones humans used, they would have all been vented into space.

Reaper didn't have time to be thankful though. His armored feet thudded along as he took the lead, passing ahead of Dirk, and shouted, "This way!" He rounded a corner in the labyrinth of corridors leading to where the *Hyperion* was docked and came face to face with another dead soldier. Before the man could raise his weapon, Reaper's highly experienced reflexes gave him the speed to put a round through the man's head. The soldier's helmet shattered as small chunks of meat and goo blew out the backside of his skull.

Reaper noticed the rookie, Peter, was right behind him. He didn't like that a bit but what was he to do? The boy was way too fresh in his unlife for him to have felt good about leaving him on the *SCAR* without being there himself to make sure Peter stayed out of trouble but now Reaper wondered if he'd made a mistake. If the boy screwed up here, they'd both die for it.

They reached the airlock at the same time as a team from one of the other two shuttles under the command of one of Reaper's most trusted warriors, Pus. Pus motioned for them to get back as he placed a charge on the airlock door leading into the *Hyperion*.

"We lost One Eye and the other team. Their shuttle didn't make it!" he yelled then darted towards where they had taken cover as the timer on the charge ticked down. A deafening explosion rocked the hallway they stood in as the airlock door imploded. Then they were all moving again, racing aboard the ship they'd came to take back with them.

A stream of the space dock's defenders caught up with them. Reaper watched the man next to Peter fall, his body nearly sawed in half by the high powered gauss rifle on the lead enemy soldier.

"Pus, I need your team to hold them!"

"Roger that!" he heard Pus shout at him as Pus spun and opened fire on the closing troops. His team fanned out, taking cover where ever they could and dug in for an extended battle if need be.

"Dirk!" Reaper screamed, "Come with me! We need your ass on the bridge getting this thing fired up yesterday!"

"Wait!" shouted Peter, "I can help."

"Then get a move on! Move it! Move it!" Reaper shouted. He knew Peter was originally from this ship. If the man had regained his memories, this could be a lot easier than they thought it was going to be.

Peter

The guy they called Pus pulled him through and sealed the outer lock and inner lock doors. "They follow us through there and the game's over."

There wasn't time to reply. Reaper was shouting.

Something still felt off inside, but for the most part, he ran smoothly, and he still knew *Hyperion* better than anyone. *She's mine. And always will be! These guys just don't know it yet!*

Dirk exited the grav tube just before him, and Reaper was on his heels. Peter led the way passing the others in a mad dash for the bridge. He knew he could access everything he needed in engineering from there.

There was little resistance aboard and Reaper and his men made short work of anyone who stood in their path. As soon as they hit the bridge, he and Dirk took over. Peter ran to the engineering console. The drive was still on board and functional. With a few key strokes, he brought it online while Dirk took the command chair.

"All systems go," Peter said. Dirk grinned at him and Peter nodded. Peter redirected the helm to the command chair. The massive ship shook as it broke free of the mooring holding it to the space dock.

"Incoming!" screamed a soldier who had taken the sensor console. "We've got fighters closing fast and two battleships breaking Earth orbit to intercept us."

Peter routed all the extra power he could into the ship's drive as Dirk pilot them away from the dock into open space.

"Is she ready?" Dirk asked.

It was Peter's turn to grin. "Oh, she's ready. Those poor guys don't have a chance." The *Hyperion's* engine was many times faster than any conventional military vessel's. She could make jumps in Leap Space at mind-boggling speed.

Dirk pressed a button and the stars blurred around them before the battleships even had a chance to get a good weapons lock on them.

El-ick

As the shuttle left the *SCAR's* bay, El-ick sat comfortably in its rear passenger compartment thinking. He was not in the slightest worried about meeting with the leaders of Centuri Prime face to face. If they made a move against him, the *SCAR* would rend their cites to shreds. There was no way the humans could recall enough vessels to match the *SCAR's* fire power fast enough to stop its rain of destruction, besides, he knew he had an ace up his sleeve. Dirk should be returning soon with the *Hyperion* and then he would have two vessels under his command in orbit around the humans' planet.

The *Hyperion* was mainly a science vessel built for exploration but like all long range ships of its era, she was also armed. She had teeth and she was super fast for a ship her size in normal space. Her Leap drive was faster still. The ship would give the humans a huge tactical advantage in the war if they could copy its drive and install similar ones on their warships.

The shuttle swooped down through Alpha Centuri Prime's atmosphere and approached the world's capital city. El-ick looked out the shuttle's window and studied the blue sky. He remembered when Earth had once looked like this place back when he was truly alive. It reminded him of the beauty that was lost when his kind took power. Their reign over the Earth was a dark one lacking the extent of personal freedoms that these humans held so dear. El-ick knew he was far more emotional than most of his race. It was both a curse and a blessing. It was part of what made him such a dangerous adversary. It was also his weakness or at least Earth Command deemed it to be. Men like Garok would never rest until they knew he was stripped of power or fell to the true death. Garok was the real reason he sent Dirk to fetch the *Hyperion* and bring it here. Stealing it out from under Garok's watch would be as much of a personal insult as it was a blow to his power base in the political arena. Garok would come for the *Hyperion*. El-ick would stake his soul on it if he could be sure he still had one.

The shuttle landed. El-ick tore himself from his thoughts and followed his two heavily armed, personal guards out to the landing platform. A group of the humans' leaders awaited him but it was the twin suns that drew his eyes. *Such beauty*, he thought. He confessed to himself that perhaps he was indeed getting soft in his old age.

A white haired man in blue robes stepped forward to meet him, extending a hand. El-ick sensed fear in him but also a determination to protect his people.

"Welcome to Alpha Centuri Prime, Admiral El-ick," the man said. "I am President Chapman, leader of the Terran Coalition, representing all the remaining worlds of man."

El-ick took his hand and shook it. "We have much to discuss and I would prefer not to do it under the rays of these suns."

President Chapman nodded. "Follow me."

The elderly man lead El-ick inside to a huge room which contained only a single table and two chairs. The President's guard remained outside as did El-ick's own.

El-ick took a seat and Chapman did the same. The old man

spoke first.

"I understand you are wanted by your people for crimes of war," the statement was clearly a question in disguise.

El-ick smirked. "You might say that. The government of my world has become corrupt and I feel it is my duty to change things. We must recapture the fires and values of our first days as a new species if my race is to survive."

"I see," Chapman said cautiously. "You do realize your presence here is likely to bring your race directly to our doorstep?"

"I do."

"Our forces are weakened and in disarray. Our ships are scattered among our colonies and many are damaged. If we give you the sanctuary you seek, we put ourselves at further risk."

"No. Your worlds would be at risk regardless. Do you not believe the dead, as you call us, will retaliate for your actions whether I am here or not? It would be foolish for you to assume they will not try to exploit your current weakness. I offer you aid in trade for shelter. I need a place where I can confront *my* enemy on my terms away from Earth and you. . . you need all the help you can get for when they come, and they will, they will come in greater force than has ever moved against your worlds at once."

"You claim you are willing to use your ship, the *SCAR*, for our defense yet it is known, even to us, that you are a humanitarian among your kind. I have heard stories of your care for your crew and those under your command."

El-ick laughed. "It will be for the greater good, will it not,

President Chapman, if I defeat my enemy and my people have a chance to truly thrive once more as we were meant to and not be ruled by fools who have only their own selfish interests at heart?"

"We would be insane to turn down your help if what you say is true. The *SCAR* alone would a great asset to any fleet. If you will defend this planet when the time comes then I will grant you the sanctuary you so desperately seek. I also ask that you keep your word and hand over the woman aboard your ship as well as the android who accompanied her home to us."

"Agreed," El-ick concluded. "I must return to the *SCAR* now. We can fine tune the terms of our agreement later. I have many things to attend to before my brethren come."

Garok

"Lord Garok," Admiral Yagsil said as his half plastic face stared at Garok from the *Rot's* veiw screen. Garok hid his disgust for the man. Yagsil had suffered major, irreversible damage to his features during the first interstellar combat with the colonies two years ago when his fighter had taken heavy fire from a human rail-gun. His entire left side was made of synthetic material. The sight made Garok sick inside. He would have ended his own life rather than display such a blatant and disgusting appearance to his peers and superiors. Garok scowled at him and waited for the Admiral to get on with it.

"The fleet is ready, my lord," Yagsil informed him. Only then did Garok smile. "Let me see it," he ordered the communications officer of *The Rot*. The screen switched to a panoramic view of space and the massive gathering of the Earth forces. Garok was happy to have Yagsil gone from his sight but even more so in what he saw on the screen.

There were four hulking troop ships, nine other battleships like *The Rot* herself, several clusters of destroyers, three fighter carriers, and too many smaller cruisers to count. He leaned into his command chair and let the majesty of the moment sink in. This time the colonies would fall. The humans had no hope left with their fleet weakened and scattered among their worlds in a desperate attempt to save as many souls as they could. Best of all though, he knew El-cik would be waiting on him. The *Hyperion* had been stolen directly from a space dock in Earth orbit. Only El-ick could manage a feat so cunning and insane. Indeed, it was that act which had allowed Garok to push those who supported him into action. He didn't truly care about the war with the humans but harvesting them would certainly be fun. All he cared about was El-ick. The fool would meet the true death as his hands and Garok knew that then and only then would his position of power would be secure. He turned to his helmsman.

"Take us to Alpha Centuri. Keep our speed to where the rest of the fleet can keep up," he added with a chuckle. The *Rot* was the most advanced in the Earth fleet. It was not as powerful or as large as the enormous monster that El-ick commanded ,but the *SCAR* was designed to be a "planet killer", breaking through a world's defenses and nuking it into the stone age. The *Rot* on the other hand was a true ship of the line. She was built for power, as well sd The *SCAR,* but a different kind of power. Her systems were designed to go head to head with other ships in direct combat. She was fast too. Until the *Hyperion's* return, she'd been the fastest known ship employed by either side in this war. As the stars blurred and she streaked into Leap Space, Garok smiled again envisioning El-ick's head before him on a pike.

El-ick

El-ick studied the data from the long range sensors via the screen on the arm of his command chair. He knew Garok would come in force but this was beyond reason even for that pompous fool. Two thirds of not just Earth Fleet but every ship controlled by the dead were less than an hour away. The humans' ragtag excuse for a fleet was gathering and preparing to leap into his sector at this very moment, but even so, they would not reach Aphla Centuri until long after the Earth forces arrived. That meant during the initial attack, the world below would only be defended by the *Griffin,* the barely repaired *Hercules*, and the exploration ship, the *Hyperion*. On the up side, the planet, being the heart of the Human Republic, was home to a thousand or more of the small fighter craft that the humans were so fond of. El-ick had demanded that the bulk of those fighters already be deployed. Every second and every shot was going to count in this opening round and he wanted to make the most of what was available to him. El-ick also had one very deadly trick up his sleeve.

The *SCAR* could more than hold her own in space combat though she was really built to destroy worlds. Her hull was covered with 80 launch tubes, each capable of firing three nukes in rapid succession. She sat among the stars with her engines primed. The second the Earth fleet leaped into the system, El-cik was going to charge them with all her guns blazing, right down their throats. The missiles would be targeted at the fleet's capital ships while the *SCAR* essentially rammed through the mass of small support vessels. The

SCAR could take the damage and survive but she would be hurt and without her primary weapons. It would reduce the fleet's numbers heavily though and should at least put them on the defensive for a matter of minutes as they regrouped. It would be up to the *Hyperion*, under Dirk's command, and the other ships to hold the line and protect the planet below at that point. The *SCAR* would be in no position to do so. El-ick hoped that with Garok in command the fleet would focus its self on the *SCAR* and not the planet until the fool made sure the *SCAR* was nothing more than space dust and he himself was dead. No matter what Garok had told the others back on Earth, El-ick knew Garok's main concern would be his demise.

Ka-Jhea

The interior of the vast underground hanger was astounding. The resources these colonies had access to must be incredible. For the moment though, the entire place was quiet, and that was a marvel in itself. She stood in a short line, third and last of the three fighter squadron leaders from the *SCAR*. Roughly a hundred and forty pilots were lined up in ranks behind her, all clad in dull black uniforms and gleaming boots. A human officer in a pure white uniform, followed by two civilians, stopped not far away. They were close enough that she saw the officer notice her.

He's actually pursing his lips while looking me over. The thought made her smile, despite the lack of respect. *Maybe he doesn't realize that I'm dead? Technically, anyway. Wonder if he has the chops to handle me, though?*

"I am General Hallachek, commander of all Terran Coalition Fighter Wings. For the moment that means I am your commander also. I am pleased to have you join us, and want to assure you that the transponders installed on your fighters will prevent any friendly fire from occurring. I am attaching your first squadron to our fighter contingent to help protect the capitol ships, including your *SCAR*, while the second and third squadrons attack their transport and drop ships. I have detached twenty *Hipper* gunships to assist your attack on the transports. We must destroy them quickly."

Hallachek paused a moment, hands on his hips. Other than a line of brass buttons on the front of his jacket and epaulets over each shoulder, his uniform was bare of decoration. *A point in his favor.*

A holstered weapon hung from the belt around his waist. Still, he didn't stand up very well when compared to El-ick.

"Any questions?" he asked at last, still looking at her.

The silence stretched out. Apparently no one had any.

"Very good, then! Let's get to our ships and prepare. Dismissed!"

She turned and ran toward her *Hades* fighter.

Garok

The *Rot* led the Earth fleet into normal space. "Holy Hell!" Garok heard his helmsman screaming. The bridge erupted into chaos. A barrage of nukes was already blazing its way across the stars towards them.

"El-ick!" Garok cursed. "Evasive maneuvers! Now!"

Only the *Rot's* super speed engines saved its destruction. The battleship's engines roared as it dropped hard below the first wave of missiles. Another wave followed hot on the heels of the first.

"Counter Measures!" Garok ordered but his weapons officer was ahead of him. The *Rot* spat interceptors at the incoming nukes as its ship to ship rail-guns opened up as well in a desperate attempt to thin the wave as a third wave bore down on it. The *Rot* took several hits before she was through the worst of the storm.

"Damage report!" Garok barked. as he stood up, gritting his teeth in anger as an explosion shook the Rot and forced him back into his command chair.

"Minor damage sir! Our armor is holding!" an officer shouted at him. "All major systems are still on line!"

"The *SCAR* is closing on us! She's approaching at ramming speed!"

What the hell? Garok stared at the massive dreadnought which filled the Rot's view screen. *Has El-ick gone mad?*

"Get us the Hell out of here!" Garok wailed.

The *Rot's* engines gave another mighty burst of power and

the *Rot* darted below the underside of the *SCAR*. It's rail-gun leaving a trail of fire across the Dreadnought as it passed.

Garok called up a view from the aft sensors. The fleet was a mess. The *SCAR's* barrage had cut it to pieces. One of the huge troop transports floated gutted, leaking energy from its engine into space and the remains of numerous battleships filled the space where the *SCAR* had torn through their lines. He couldn't even guess at the losses inflicted on the smaller vessels that the dreadnought had plowed directly into.

"Sir!" an officer shouted. "We have three human ships breaking orbit from the planet. They're moving on an intercept course."

Garok looked up at the Rot's main screen. The ships looked as if they were in some kind of cloud. "Magnification." he ordered. The image became clearer. "My God," he breathed. The cloud wasn't a problem with the Rot's sensors at all. It was a swarm of fighters the likes of which Garok had never seen before.

"Have the fleet launch all fighters. Tell the them to cover the transports. I want troops on the ground as quickly as possible." Garok whirled to face his comm officer, his eyes burning with anger and hatred. "Order every remaining capital ship to target the *SCAR*. I want to see it burn in nuclear fire."

"Y-Y-Yes sir," the comm officer stammered under the heat of Garok's rage.

"I'm coming for you El-ick," Garok whispered. "Helmsman! Bring us around. Engage the *SCAR*. All weapons, FIRE!"

Ron

The troops they gave him were all recruits, barely out of Basic Training. They had no experience at all. Ron found himself in command of the entire southern ground defense for the capital city of New Charlotte. In desperation he promoted Chad to sergeant. The man had been one before, and was rumored to have a volcanic temper if provoked. Ron had never seen any of that., just a relaxed hard working guy. In the last year he worked so long with the man that they thought alike when it came to tactics despite their differences outside of uniform.

Five hundred men surrounded the tiny outpost which once the two of them had manned on their own. If the dead dropped ferals into the desert beyond the city, the monsters were certainly going to be in for a fight if they tried to reach it below. Ron stood on top of the outpost's roof scanning the night sky with his binoculars. No sun to blind his men and that gave them an advantage. They'd easily be able to see any pods the ships in space launched at the planet's surface and be able to move to intercept them. Ron knew the deciding battle for the fate of Alpha Centuri was the one being fought among the stars but it was his job to protect the civilian population down here in the sand and it was one he took very seriously. He would carry out his orders until his dying breath.

A streak of orange shot through the darkness above. He knew instantly what it was. Falling like a meteorite, the pod crashed into the sand miles beyond the perimeter he'd established around the city. It smashed into the earth like a bomb. Even from where he stood, Ron could see the impact through his powerful binoculars. It was a tried and true dead tactic. The pods hit with enough force to do a world of damage on their own. If some of the ferals inside met the true death or were injured too badly to be of any use as shock troops, it was no great loss to the dead forces. It was a certainty that enough of the creatures would make it through the impact to wreck havoc and spread the disease they carried to human populace. Their numbers would grow with every death they caused, more than enough to make up for any lost when the pod impacted.

Ron's breath caught in his chest as a second pod appeared in the sky, then another, and another. He lost count after the fiftieth lit up the sky. It wasn't their numbers that frightened him though, it was the direction the pods were falling. They weren't aimed at the desert. They were aimed at New Charlotte herself. He watched as explosions from the impact of the pods rocked the great city. Flames rose and spread through her streets and from the carters where the pods crashed, the dead flowed forth into her streets. It was unimaginable. Something was terribly wrong. The orbital defenses should have stopped any pods on a trajectory which took them into the city but clearly that was not happening. Either the defenses were destroyed or disabled and the city herself was vulnerable to direct attack from space. Almost every single soldier on the surface was stationed somewhere along the perimeter under Ron's command. There was no one beyond the normal law enforcement personnel left inside New Charlotte to confront or hold back the hordes of flesh eating monsters which were now running amok in the city proper. Ron glanced at Chad and saw the man must be thinking the same thing. "Order everyone to fall back to New Charlotte!" he yelled. "We have to get down there or we won't have a city to defend!"

"Too late, sir. They're too close. I think we're going to have to face them."

"I think you're right, Sergeant."

Claudia

Admiral El-ick had kept his word. He'd released Frank and her to the authorities of Alpha Centuri Prime as soon as the Human Republic agreed to his terms. A shuttle from the SCAR had transported them to the surface. They'd been through grueling hours of questions from the government, med scans to make sure they weren't being used as a means to infect the populace of New Charlotte with the dead virus, and finally what seemed like endless hours addressing the world's press. Some of the reporters questions were worse than the ones posed by the government due to their extremely personal nature. One man had gone so far as to ask if she and Frank were sleeping together despite the fact that Frank was now a walking mass of open metal and looked every inch the android that he was. After all the hoopla with the press was over with, she and Frank had been assigned two soldiers who acted as their "personal guards" so they could go out into the city and see how mankind had changed since the fall of Earth. Though their value was great to the leadership of the Human Republic as they had direct intel on what Earth was like now, Claudia knew the guards were there just as much to keep an eye on them as they were there for their protection.

Claudia took Frank to a diner that called itself "The Oasis in the Sand" which served many old style Earth foods. As she and Frank sat at the table discussing their ordeal and their new found freedom, their two guards waited outside the establishment on the street keeping an eye on them through the plexi-glass window beside their table. Claudia shoved a fork of something that was supposed to be fish, but tasted more like chicken, into her mouth as Frank expressed his sincere apologies for the fourth time on being unable to tell her what he was during their years about the Hyperion. Regulations had demanded he keep his presence secret so he could watch over the Hyperion's human compliment for any signs of space born dementia due to the extremely long length of their mission. He would also serve as an "ace in the hole" should the need arise.

Suddenly Frank stopped in mid-sentence as he was still droning on about the reasons of his secrecy. The pupils of his robotic eyes dilated wider and his expression shifted as much as it was possible given his current condition from one of concern to one of fear. "Get down!" he screamed at her, yanking her from her chair onto the floor underneath their table with as an explosion boomed on the street outside. Shards of glass blew inward from where the window had been and clattered across the top of their table. Frank stood up, knocking over the table which had been their shield in the process. Claudia watched him closely. "It's safe for the moment," he informed her, "Our guards are dead. I suggest we secure the weapons they carried and seek a more secure place of shelter."

Claudia got to her feet staring out into the street beyond. It looked as if the dead had bombed this portion of the city. At the end of the main road between the stores and apartments lining the sides of the streets sat a massive metal sphere, halfway buried into the ground.

"Is that what hit us?" she asked Frank.

"I believe so," Frank confirmed, "I do not believe it truly detonated or we would no longer exist."

"Uh, Frank. . ." she said as they watched the sphere together, "I don't think it's a bomb."

The top of the sphere burst open and dozens upon dozens of rotting, bleeding monsters emerged from it. They poured out of it like a swarm of bees from a hive. Their howls of hunger and rage filled the night.

She felt Frank take her arm. "We must go now Claudia," he said and shoved her towards the restaurant's entrance which led out onto the street. "Run!" his metallic voice screamed as a dead man from the pod spotted them and shook his head wildly slinging saliva and blood through the air as he howled at them and started in their direction at a full on sprint.

Frank snatched up a rifle which had belonged to one of their guards, who's cooked and broken body lay near them. and opened up at the man. The rifle's bullets traced a line from his stomach to his head on full auto as Frank found his aim. The last rounds of Frank's shot blew the man's head apart like it was an overripe melon. His decaying form crumpled to the street with a thud. Eight more of the things took his place charging at them. Frank told her to run again, lowering his rifle and following after her. Claudia spun on her heels and took off with her legs pumping as hard as they could.

They rounded the corner and came face to face with a hover car hauling ass down the road towards them. Frank shoved Claudia from its path but didn't have time to dodge it himself. It slammed into him like an old Earth train tossing him through the air into the window of a nearby shop. The car spun out of control and vanished around the corner, disappearing from view. Claudia scrambled to her feet. "Frank!"

Frank emerged from the shop, stumbling towards her. One metal arm was folded over his stomach area. Claudia raced to him. "Are you ok?"

Frank looked up at as if it took him a moment to notice she was there. "I have sustained damage to some of my internal systems including my power supply."

He removed the hand covering his stomach and Claudia saw a large dent where his metal was pressed inward from the impact with the car. There were cracks which leaked a black oil like fluid intermingled with something that looked very much like blood. She had no idea if it were real or synthetic. "I am afraid I have lost our only weapon," he informed her in a monotone voice. "This may prove to be rather a problem."

"Can you run?" she asked.

"Yes. However at my current rate of power leakage, I have hours at best until I shutdown completely."

Claudia wondered if Frank could die. Would who he was be lost if he shutdown or would his mind lay dormant in something akin to human sleep until he could be repaired?

"Come on Frank!" she said reaching out to help him as a pack of howling dead creatures came sprinting around the corner of the road at them. "We have to move!"

Ka-Jhea

She could feel a thin sheen of sweat at her temples and upper lip as her flight of fighters and gunships finally broke through the atmosphere of New Charlotte and into true space. Sometimes it seemed that her body was still trying to reject the alien presence that now maintained it, while at other times, a happy medium was reached. Sweating was a welcome, normal procedure for cooling that she embraced and was grateful for. It was also a reminder that she was under stress and needed to be careful.

Her collection of forty some-odd fighters and five gunships were rapidly approaching one of the already orbiting troopships. Any moment now, she knew, the first rank of pods ranked upon the colossal ship would begin to drop like overripe fruit from a tree. *We need to destroy them before that happens. Catch 'em still on vine so to speak.*

There was no sign of protective fighters as she streaked in, already lining up for her first run. She flicked the safety off for her guns and slid her fingers around the duel triggers.

"Good hunting, and look out for each other. See you on the other side."

There were one or two grunts in reply, but nothing to indicate that any of them cared whether she lived or died.

Concentrate, take deep breathes. The target wavered. Sweat rolled into her right eye. The release mechanism for an entire row of pods lay exposed and surrounded by the targeting cue. She pressed down on the triggers, hosing the machinery in a hail of explosive, uranium-tipped rounds. Before her a brief but enveloping flare of light obscured her view.

The troop ship was still there but it looked like one whole row of pods were stuck. Right behind her the rest of her ships followed, launching missiles and firing their own guns.

Several defensive guns opened up, and three of her comrades vanished when the heavy bore guns scored hits on their ships. One of the *Hipper* gunships was caught in a crossfire from two different defensive batteries and came apart in a white hot cloud of molten debris.

She circled around for another run, concentrating again, trying to aim. Flinching each time a piece of wreckage buffeted her ship.

Ron

The mingled rays of the two suns had just touched the horizon. The smell of rot, spilled bowels and vomit were heavy in his nose.

"Duck!" Chad yelled, and Ron threw himself flat on the sand.

Chad cut lose with an extended burst from the grenade launcher. He tracked from left to right, each grenade tossing bodies in the air, shredding and slashing the onrushing horde, but not slowing it.

Ron glanced at the man beside him: one of the green recruits. He hadn't wanted to leave the boy behind. Boy was correct. He couldn't be more than fifteen. Fifteen, but wearing the uniform of a soldier. Someone, or something shot him. The wound was high on his back, just about centered between his shoulder blades. No exit would was on the other side.

Right now a bloody froth was draining from between the boy's clenched teeth. Sand clung and caked to his face and neck.

The howls rose and grew closer. The grenade launcher fell silent. "I'm out, sir!" screamed Chad. "Everyone else is dead."

Ron climbed to his knees, ready to lift the boy back over his shoulder. He found himself nearly face to face with the boy and just about gagged. His eyes were open, opague, filmed over and blinking. *He passed over! He's dead!*

Ron threw himself backwards, crabbing away, even as the thing stirred into motion following him. Both got to their feet at the same time. The now feral boy leapt at him, hands outstretched, and

Ron stepped to the left and threw a right cross at the kid's jaw. Terrible pain exploded from the impact of his hand. Might have broke a knuckle.

The undead thing dropped to a knee, and Ron didn't hesitate to draw his combat knife and stab. The blade's point went into the thing's eye to the hilt. He tried to yank it free as it fell over but the handle slipped through his fingers. The newly dead, or dead again body slid to the ground.

"Run Captain!" shouted Chad. "There was a convoy in route to us, just a mile or so north of that hill. Heard a lot of shooting and explosions there not long ago, but maybe we'll find help."

Ron looked at the Chad's face, "Okay, Chad, lead on!"

El-ick

"Forward armor has been compromised in numerous locations!" El-ick heard one his bridge crew shouting. Sparks flew all around him as he sat in his command chair.

"All nukes expended!" his weapons officer informed him.

"We're taking heavy fire to port sir! *Rot* is making another strafing run!"

"The other ships?" El-ick asked calmly amid the storm of chaos.

"The remaining four battleships of the fleet are closing behind us! The aft armor is failing in sections. We have hull breaches on all sides!"

El-ick smiled darkly in the dim light of the bridge. He knew the *SCAR* could take all this damage and more. Its massive size rendered it very hard to destroy and it was unlikely that any major systems would be knocked fully off line.

"Target the *Rot*. Bring all rail-guns within range to bare on her," he ordered.

"Sir?" The weapons officer asked. "What about the other battleships?"

"Now," El-ick said again in a tone that left no room for disagreement.

The *Rot* was the only real threat to the ship. The *Rot's* advanced systems and speed gave it as much as an edge as the *SCAR's* mass gave it. It had to be taken out of play before it could do any serious damage beyond what the *SCAR* had already suffered.

The *SCAR's* hull was littered with weak spots from the impacts of the hundreds of smaller vessels it had plowed through moments before. If Garok could figure out which ones to exploit, they were in very real trouble.

Another barrage of combined fire from the closing battleships struck the SCAR. The communications station to El-ick left exploded, sending its operator rolling across the floor in flames. The crew of the *SCAR* had never faced this level of damage or threat before. The ship had always been an unstoppable juggernaut since she'd first left space dock. El-ick was proud of the way they were holding up against the fear and pressure of the risk they were taking, almost single-handedly tackling the entire Earth fleet by themselves.

The *SCAR's* entire port battery of rail-guns opened at the *Rot.* The sleek battleship dodged most of the fire but took a few good hits to its side as it passed by. It blazed on into the stars before turning to make another run at the *SCAR.*

El-ick was well aware that Garok would not make a suicide run against him. Garok was far too much of a coward and greedy for the spoils he hoped to gain upon El-ick's death to end his own life. Yet such a threat did exist from the other ships under his command. With the *SCAR's* now limited array of weapons at its disposal, El-ick doubted he could fend off such an attack if Garok ordered it. El-ick shifted in his chair. "What is the status of the planet?"

"The troop transports have managed to launch hundreds of pods into the atmosphere despite our fighters attempts to stop them. The *Hyperion* and the other ships have prevented the remaining destroyers and cruisers to obtain orbital barrage positions however."

El-ick weighed his options as the *Rot* darted by the *SCAR,* this time flying over her and unleashing a stream of nukes directly into her top side. The explosion were so many and so vast he felt their impact even on the bridge. As the *Rot* streaked away, The *SCAR's* rail-guns fired tracer rounds after her. El-ick watched as they finally managed to score a well placed hit. The *Rot* lurched hard to starboard as one her three aft engines blew in an eruption of flame and radiation before flickering out. She floundered in space for a moment, taking fire from The *SCAR*, before she righted herself and began a new series of evasive maneuvers. This maneuver allowed her to escape the pounding she was taking.

At her best, the *SCAR* could have dealt with five battleships, even if one of them was The Rot, however she was far from at her best. Her missiles were spent and she had taken a great deal of damage.

"Bring us about," El-ick ordered his helmsman. "Give the general order to abandon ship."

"Sir?" His communications officer asked looking as if he surely must have heard El-ick wrong.

"Give the order to abandon ship. I will not see anymore of this crew die fighting my battle for me. Garok is my responsibility alone."

The look in El-ick's eyes was hard and cold as watched the officer at the Com Station to make sure the order was carried out. El-ick turned to his the bridge's engineering officer. "Route all systems to my control," he said taping some keys on the arm of his command chair.

Klaxons blared throughout the *SCAR* as its crew raced for the shuttles in the massive ship's hangar bays and spherical escape pods were jettisoned into space from every level of the ship. El-ick switched the *SCAR's* rail-guns into a defensive mode, covering the vessels of his fleeing crew. Somewhere aboard the *Rot* he imagined Garok was wondering what in the devil he was up to. A smile split his full lips as he watched the *Rot* coming around at *SCAR* once more. Very few in all of Earth Command knew the true extent of the *SCAR's* maneuverability. While she was certainly no match for a ship like The Rot, she was insanely quick for a ship her size. The *Rot* swooped in and El-ick keyed a command into the re-routed helm controls. The *SCAR* lurched as all her engines fired at once and took her directly into The *Rot's* path. The *Rot* had no time to veer off. The battleship smashed into the forward side of the *SCAR*. The *Rot's* speed drove her into the *SCAR* like a needle before she exploded taking a good fourth of the *SCAR* with her. El-ick felt the coldness of space leaking onto the bridge around him. The *SCAR's* internal light atmosphere was long vented in the stars. It was only a matter of minutes until the residual heat was gone as well and he froze solid where he sat. He checked the status of the weapon systems. Forty percent of the *SCAR's* rail-guns were still functional although with the crew gone, their ammo would be expended in seconds. The remaining four battleships were holding off. They'd even ceased firing as if too stunned to take action. El-ick cursed as his continued systems check revealed the *SCAR's* engines were off line. He was a sitting duck and unable to take the fight to them. He had only one option left. El-ick punched in a series of commands and the *SCAR's* rail-guns emptied their remaining ammo at the battleships. They all took several hits. It was just enough to stir their captains to anger once more, just as El-ick had hoped. Their engines flared and they streaked toward the *SCAR* with all guns blazing. The impacts of missiles blowing large chunks from the *SCAR's* battered remains and the constant stream of rail-gun fire punching holes through the remnants of its armor filled El-ick with a sense of rapture. The sounds of destruction were like a symphony to him. Ice had formed over parts of his body and his legs were already frozen solid. His hand snapped and popped with the noise of breaking tendons and tearing muscles as he lifted it just enough to hit the last key needed to initiate the pre-programmed sequence he'd prepared. As his finger stabbed the button he tried to laugh but there was no air. This was a fitting end to his new "life". It had been one of death and the art of war from the moment he rose back up to be one of the dead when the virus first struck the population of Earth.

The *SCAR* exploded like a super nova as the battleships closed in on it. Two of them were vaporized by the blast. The next closest took heavy damage barely managing to turn in time to escape the fate of the first two. The final battleship which had been the furthest back was spun like a top into the void, trying to right itself as the concussive wave of the blast pushed on.

Peter

Peter stood at the engineering station on the bridge of the *Hyperion* behind the command chair. He watched the events unfolding on the view screen over Dirk's shoulder. The darkness of space was lit by a massive explosion as the *SCAR* blew itself to pieces, taking most of the remaining enemy capital ships with it. Dirk was screaming orders and the bridge was in a state of chaos. The *Hyperion*, like the other two battleships fighting for the survival of Alpha Centuri Prime, was being swarmed by *Hades* fighters. The small craft flew all around it blasting holes in its armor as the *Hyperion's* rail-guns blazed away in continuous streams of shifting fire trying to fend them off.

Peter knew they had the advantage now. Though they were still outnumbered, the dead's cruisers and few remaining destroyers were no match for them. It was only a matter of time until they forced the dead into a full on retreat or destroyed them. A cheer rose up as several groups of human fighters swooped in, driving off the bulk of the swarm attacking the ship. Of course, he knew too that the greatest threat left from the dead were the hulking troop transports which continued to launch burst after burst of shock troop pods at the planet below.

"We have to take out those transports!" Dirk raged. "Maximum speed!"

Peter poured more power to the engines as the helmsman closed the distance between the *Hyperion* and the closest of the two transports. The *Hyperion* was far from a t rue battleship. She did sport super heavy armor and that was the main thing that kept her alive during the course of the battle which raged around her. Her weapons were nothing to laugh at but very limited. Most of them were defensive in nature due to her being an exploration vessel. None the less, she blazed her way across space towards the transport.

"Peter?" he heard Dirk call out.

"She's down to her last eight nukes," Peter answered.

"Then we better make them count," Dirk said turning to stare at the weapon's officer. "Launch six at that transport as soon as you get a clear shot!"

Six daggers trailing fire spat from the *Hyperion's* forward missile tubes. Not a single one reached their target. A wave of *Hades* fighters came out of no where, intercepting the attack. They were quickly met and engaged by a group of fighters who hailed from the *SCAR* as the *Hyperion* streaked on passed leaving the two groups in its wake.

"One more shot!" Peter warned.

"No," Dirk shook his head and turned to face Peter. "Two nukes aren't going to take that monster out. I need options."

Peter knew the *Hyperion* better than anyone else living or dead and now it came down to him to save the day. He wasn't a hero or even a warrior despite his newly acquired post death training. He was an engineer and always would be. His mind searched over everything the *Hyperion* had left in its nearly depleted arsenal and found nothing that would do the job. Then it hit him. He smiled and looked Dirk in the eye. "I have a plan but it's risky. It will endanger this ship and everyone aboard."

"Peter," Dirk warned him.

"Right," Peter said feeling stupid. There were all already at risk. This was a war after all. "Rerouting helm controls to the engineering station. Don't panic. I am going to need to put us literally on top of that transport."

Dirk shot him a look that told him to get on it with it. The look quickly became one of fear as he watched Peter steer the *Hyperion* up into a docking position as it approached the transport.

If the troop carrier had been better armed, they would've been blown to space dust as Peter brought the hull of the *Hyperion* within inches of the transport's hull. Peter channeled every ounce of available power left into the Hyperion's Leap drive and activated it. When a ship emerged from Leap space it created a very close proximity small scale explosion. Peter was counting on the reverse happening here and in theory, it was possible. A Leap bubble formed around the ship, slicing through the armored hull of the transport and sucking large chunks of the vessel into Leap space along with the *Hyperion*. Peter imagined he could hear the screech of the metal tearing before the Hyperion leapt away and the transport exploded milliseconds after the *Hyperion* vanished.

The *Hyperion* dropped out Leap space a good distance away from the battle but still close enough to be within visual range of it. He caught a glimpse of what was happening around Alpha Centuri before the cracked view screen went black. The other battleships had finished off the rest of the dead and were in the process of mopping up the last of their fighters and small cruisers as they tried to flee.

The *Hyperion* was in rough shape. The ship's power was depleted and she floated lifeless among the stars amid the debris she'd carried with her. Systems were shorting out all over the bridge as the backwash of the leap caught up with them. No ship was designed to pull another into Leap space with them and doing so had cost them even more than Peter had bargained for. He watched as the bridge's ceiling bulked and gave way from the stress of the re-entry. A jagged piece of metal flew from the exploding helm controls and planted itself directly in Dirk's forehead. The captain slumped forward in chair as the true death claimed him. Peter took over, barking orders, as he raced to stir the rest of the crew into action before the ship was fully lost. He tied what was left of the ship's internal sensors into the controls of the engineering station and began to coordinate the damage control teams being hastily assembled throughout the ship.

"Are you taking over command?" asked a voice over his shoulder.

"Yes, just hold onto whatever you want for a moment or two more."

Two minutes later, Peter turned in the chair to look at the man behind him.

The man standing before him was a short slim guy who always took Dirk's orders without comment or question. He hadn't recognized him at first because half of the man's face was beet red, like he had a bad sunburn. The gell coating his skin was dried and cracked where he'd been burned. A moment later, recognition came, "You are the helmsman."

"Yes, I am Hatron, helmsman and second officer."

"What did you want to ask me?"

"Whether you were taking over command."

Peter hesitated, looking around the bridge area. Several crewman stood or sat at their posts, all apparently waiting for his answer.

"Yes, I am."

Hatron nodded, "Very good sir. What are your orders?"

Claudia

Claudia raced through the streets of New Charlotte with Frank at her side. They'd been on the run for a while now and the exertion was beginning to take its toll on Frank. The android was moving more slowly and his level of lucidity seemed to come and go. Sometimes he would babble to himself as they ran, chanting a series of numbers that sounded like some sort of binary code. Claudia knew the leak in his power cell was shutting him down and all the energy they were forced to expend was only making it worse. They couldn't stop though, not if they wanted to stay alive. The dead were everywhere. Everyone the dead killed got up and joined their ranks causing their numbers to grow at an exponential rate.

Claudia kept up her frantic pace, trying to find somewhere, anywhere, safe. Her legs pumped beneath her and her hair was drenched with sweat. Her breath came in ragged gasps as she pushed herself on. People were screaming over the howls of the feral dead. She saw a man to her right being dragged from a store through its front window. There were three of the creatures tearing at him and trying to pull him apart so that they could share his flesh. To her left, a naked man who's back was covered deep cuts, that no longer bled, sat on his haunches and gnawed on the arm of a beautiful woman in expensive looking garb. The woman was still alive though all her limbs were missing. Her wet eyes met Claudia's in a silent plea as tears streamed down her cheeks. Claudia turned her eyes away.

"Look out!" she heard Frank yell at her. She barely managed

to fling herself to the side as a man, missing most of the skin on his chest and smeared with blood not his own, leaped out at her from an alleyway as they passed it. Claudia lost her balance and thudded to the ground as Frank moved in on the man. Frank grabbed him, lifting him into the air with a single hand, and slammed him so hard into the metal wall of the building beside them that she heard the man's bones snap like twigs. Frank tossed the man aside and offered Claudia a hand up. She took it, noticing that one of Frank's eyes had gone dark. She started to ask him about it but he cut her off. "That large warehouse is our closest hope of secure shelter," he informed her.

Together they sprang forward again. Claudia's heart pounded in her chest as they covered the remaining distance to it. The building's huge doors were locked when she tried them.

"Step aside," Frank ordered her. An interface device popped out of his wrist like the blade of a switchblade. He plunged it into the control panel beside the door and his good eye closed as if he were no longer inside the metal form which stood beside her. A moment later Frank opened his eye at the same time the door slid inward allowing them entrance. As soon as they were inside it closed behind them. There were no lights. The interior of the warehouse was as dark as a cloudy and starless night.

"What is this place?" Claudia asked.

"It is a storage facility currently owned by the Earth historical preservation society according to what I could learn from the computer. Come on!" Frank said darting off into the shadows, his heavy feet clanging on the metal of the floor. "I believe I have found our means of escape."

Without warning one of the servo motors in his left leg stopped functioning and Claudia watched him fall, skidding across the floor to come to rest a few feet from the large tarp covered object he'd been leading her towards.

"Frank!" she cried out and rushed to him. She leaned over him as he looked up at her with eyes that were now totally dark.

"This is where I leave you Claudia." His voice was weak and slurred.

"No, Frank. There's gotta to be something in here we can use to repair you. Jury rig you a new power source."

With a visible effort, the android shook his head. "If the warehouse's data files are correct the key should be in something referred to as the "glove box". God speed, Claudia Coyne."

Frank's head dropped to the floor and his body lay motionless.

"Damn you, Frank," she cursed through her tears. She stood and jerked the tarp off the vehicle it covered. She couldn't help but laugh as she saw the brilliant, red chrome of the car's hood. If she remembered her old Earth history correctly this sort of model was called a Barchetta. There wasn't a door so she hopped inside. Her eyes scanned the car's interior looking for a box but didn't see one. Finally, she noticed a small closed compartment in front of the passenger seat. Inside were the keys just like Frank had told her. She stuck them in the ignition and the engine roared to life. Revving it a few times to make sure it worked she floored the gas. The tires spun out, squealing, as the car hurled itself towards the door they'd entered through. It slid open as she approached and knew it doing so was Frank's work. He must have preprogrammed it to be ready for their means of escape. The Barchetta bounced into the street. Claudia swerved to avoid a pack of creatures charging towards her, jerking the wheel hard to the left. She righted the car, narrowly avoiding crashing into a restaurant at the edge of the road. Wind blew through her hair as she picked up speed and drove onward towards the edge of New Charlotte and the desert beyond. Getting out of the city was the main priority. If she survived doing that, she'd figure out what came next later.

The airport isn't too far from here. Just follow the road.

Ron

The sky was gray. Sometime in the last hour or so, the wind picked up bringing with it towering storm clouds, but no relief from the heat of the twin suns overhead.

Ron paused and leaned over, his breathing ragged and uneven.

Most of the re-supply column was burning. Only two vehicles out of twenty were still intact. Thousands of bodies littered the cratered ground surrounding the road. In a near hopeless last stand the officer commanding the column had called down an artillery strike on the position. Too late to save anyone though. Everyone died.

"These MAC's are great," said Chad, referring to the tracked tank-like vehicle he was sitting in. MAC was short for Mobile Armored Carrier.

Ron didn't reply. He hefted the heavy box of ammunition onto his shoulder and handed it up to the man sitting up in the turret.

"That's eight boxes," said Chad, lowering the box onto the tray beside him. "I just need to link this one up and feed it into the well and we're ready." He patted the 30mm cannon barrel. "We'll be packing quite a wallop with this baby on full-auto sir."

"Good," Ron answered, grabbing his Assault Multi-Purpose, or AMP, rifle from where it leaned against the vehicle. Someone was approaching.

A haggard-looking sergeant limped over to the two men. On his left arm was the brassard of the military police. "I'm Sergeant-

Major Rudd and I've got four men left. Can we hitch a ride, sir?"

"That's up to you Sergeant-Major. We're heading back to the capitol. Sure could use your help."

The Sergeant-Major turned around and made a waving motion with his right hand. Four shapes rose from the ground and ran towards them.

"Where'd you guys come from, sir?" Rudd asked.

"We came from Sarhaggen Point, the outpost over-looking the desert."

Rudd looked shocked, "Just you and him, sir? That's ten miles from here."

"There may be other survivors, but my men were green, Sergeant! Most died in the second wave of attacks we faced."

Rudd's face went stony, and he raised his AMP rifle, centering it on Ron's chest. "You a deserter Captain?"

"What if we both are, Sergeant?" asked Chad from his perch up in the turret of the MAC. He held a pistol aimed at the military policeman.

"Guess we'd have a problem then, Private."

"And if we aren't deserters?" Ron asked, watching the man swallow.

"Well, sir, we really have no proof of you doing anything but your duty. I'd like to apologize for jumping to conclusions."

"What do you say to that, Private Morris?" Ron asked Chad. "Think he's sincere?"

Chad grinned. "You told him earlier that we needed help sir.

I'd say let them pile into the back of the MAC and let's go. People are dying as we speak."

"Pile in then, Sergeant, and we'll get out of here."

The man gave a shaky grin in return, and then followed his men through the hatch in the back.

Taking a chance on that one. But was there a choice anyway?

Reaper

From above, the scale of the buildings and the light monorail that linked the entire complex of Braxton Airport to the capitol of New Charlotte, was quite impressive. Reaper did his best to memorize all he could until the moment the shuttles set down.

The survivors from the *SCAR* all landed en mass on the tarmac of the civilian spaceport two kilometers from the capitol's environs. Reaper's marines formed a perimeter and even now were engaging ferals. The rest of the crew was armed but weren't trained for this type of combat. Better to get them into a secure building and use the marines for anything else.

"Most of the capitol is burning sir," said one of his grizzled veterans. He couldn't remember the man's name at the moment, but noticed that the man was hunchbacked and missing an ear.

"Gather a squad and I will clear the terminal building. Might be able to use that monorail to ferry survivors out of the city. Otherwise we'll be fighting our own kind for a long time."

"Right away, sir," the man replied and turned away.

Reaper took a moment to check his rifle over and to test draw his knife a few times. No telling when or where he would need to use a blade, but it was well-used.

He began to walk towards the terminal. It looked like a fragile piece of human confectionary, all airy spaces, glass and ribbon-thin steel supports, but he knew it could withstand quite a bit of punishment. Small arms certainly weren't a threat.

On the inside he could see that quite a few refugees must

have sought shelter here. The only problem must have been no one to protect them. Somehow the ferals got inside. Blood smeared many of the windows. Violated, eviscerated bodies lay sprawled everywhere inside. Most weren't moving.

He wanted to feel something but the most he could muster was a dim memory of his own near blind bloodlust. Only the combat itself engaged him now. Slaughter and feasting were for the ferals.

For the mindless killing machines.

The nameless veteran came up behind him, followed by nine more marines.

"We'll go in right here, at the main entrance. Take point," Reaper said, pointing at the veteran.

The man nodded and stepped through the shattered doors. He held his weapon ready. Ferals weren't the only worry. Quite often they were accompanied by snipers and other types of specialist soldier that could complement their mass attack style.

The rest of the squad followed with Reaper walking in the middle. They entered a cavernous lobby. At the far side were ticket counters and concourses branching off to the various terminal buildings. In the midst of all this, the slaughter was still underway.

Reaper's men began to fire, taking out each feral using as few rounds possible.

Bodies began to rise all around them, some half-eaten, while others wore the mottled-pattern desert camouflage he was used to associating with his own side.

Moments later all was still in the lobby. Reaper's men paused a moment to re-load, then when they were ready, he dispatched them in pairs , to clear each area.

Somehow, when they were all dispatched, the hunchbacked soldier was still there with him. "Come with me. We'll take the tower."

They came to a service door marked, "Authorized Personnel Only."

"This is the way, sir," the man said, and tried the door.

It was unlocked and opened inwards. They entered a long passageway.

"What's your name, soldier?" Reaper asked.

"Most people call me Hunch, sir."

"Do you remember your real name?"

The man turned back toward Reaper and stared. "What does it matter?" he snapped. "I'm a good soldier and follow orders, don't I?"

"Better tone it down, soldier, or I'll rip your head off."

"I was a scientist, sir, doing important work. I wasn't a soulless undead killer. I lived, loved and lost. Your people took my only reasons for living and turned me into this...this thing that craves the most hideous things."

"You are remembering quite a bit, then." Reaper's voice was soft.

"My name was Norman Botts, sir."

Reaper looked at the man. "Well Norman, we get each other through this, and I'll see what I can do to get you back to your work.

We are forging something new here with our enemies."

For a moment or two, Botts looked him in the eye. "It's too late, sir, but it was a nice offer. We need to clear this building now before it is too late to save anyone."

They were mere steps from the end of the passage. Botts turned away and reached for the door. Reaper noticed a high-heeled shoe in the corner, against the wall. The door opened and a horde of ferals poured out. Botts didn't scream, but he made a mewling sound as one of them shoved a hand into his mouth. Another leaned in and bit deeply into his throat. The weight of the bodies literally bore Botts backward and knocked him down. The ferals poured over him and some were already trying to get to Reaper.

He opened fire, emptying a full magazine of fifty explosive bullets into the mass of flesh, then he pulled a grenade off of his harness. While backpedaling, he removed the pin, counted to three and tossed it. The concussion nearly blew out his eardrums and tossed him to the ground. Grisly fragments showered down on him.

While lying on his back, he licked at the blood on his lips. Nothing moved while he lay there. Nothing reacted as he got to his feet either. He could see Botts' face beneath a tangle of charred limbs and torsos. There was a peaceful quality there now.

Wonder if I'll look like that someday?

Reaper re-loaded his rifle, slung it over his back and pulled his knife. The blade was almost 12 cm long and was double-edged. He stepped on the bodies and crossed into the stairwell beyond. *Just need to finish the job now.*

Peter

"We are on course for the last two transports, sir," said Hatron. "We have little more than our small caliber anti-fighter emplacements to attack with."

"Thank you, Hatron," Peter said, feeling a bit awkward. The man needed a rank.

"Do you have a rank?"

"I am Lieutenant, sir."

"Very good. It looks like our forces are already attacking the transports, Lieutenant."

"They are. That is Ka-Jhea's squadron, sir."

Ka-Jhea. I have heard of her but can't remember seeing her. Just a name. With Claudia, he could still feel or at least remember something of what it felt like to love, to feel the blood move in your veins.

He remembered their last encounter in the Virtual World. *Never really made up for that. Too proud. Too eager to prove that I didn't need anyone. The sex was good. Even she would admit that. Just that damn Frank ruined it. Wonder if either of them made it? My curiosity won't let me be at peace.*

I have to know.

"We do what we can here, Lieutenant, then we see about New Charlotte."

"Yes sir."

The two immense ships came into view on the main display. A cloud of fighters surrounded the transports as the second one began to launch pods   On a secondary display off to his right, Peter watched as the anti-fighter guns began to open fire on the pods. Each gun was dual-barreled, and capable of 'lock-in' fire.   This meant that the guns could track and attempt to second guess what the pilot would do.   Vindication for bringing them into play was immediate as several pods exploded, scattering bodies and debris over a wide area.

Peter spotted a single *Hades* fighter braving the gauntlet of fire and debris. The fighter juked to the side, narrowly avoiding the transport's defensive fire, and launched a torpedo.

Peter said a prayer.

Claudia

The car literally flew across the desert. The lack of a windshield made her keep her eyes squinted to slits, but the wind, the speed and the heat all were a potent medicine for melancholy.

She almost by-passed the turn-off for the spaceport but forced herself to slow down and take the turn. There were immediate signs that this might not have been the best idea, but she was stubborn. The remains of a pod lay less than a hundred yards to the right of the road and the only signs of life she saw were a pair of vultures circling the wreck.

A slow but loud rumble of thunder crashed somewhere overhead. No rain or lightning. She rounded a corner and the spaceport was there. Small spacecraft were everywhere, most of them of the same make, military shuttles painted black with a streak of red. *The SCAR! They must have sent help down!*

As she drew closer, the sound of explosions and gunfire reached her. In the distance an entire hanger exploded sending a roiling cloud of oily smoke skyward.

With no real plan, she allowed the car to drift to a stop near one of the shuttles.

A moment later marines from the *SCAR* surrounded her car.

"Please exit the vehicle."

She got out.

Ka-Jhea

Fuel's almost gone. The thought meant next to nothing. Just a statistic. Might have enough for one last try.

All around her, her companions were being destroyed. Few would escape this attack, but if they failed, then escaping wasn't possible anyway. The torpedoes the Hades fighters always carried were rarely used. The range was so short, they were close to a suicide weapon. To get close enough took nerves of steel and a lot of luck.

She apparently had both.

Her first torpedo went right in to one of the armored exhausts of the already damaged transport. More than half of its pods were still attached.

Ka-Jhea banked sharply up, out and away to the port side of the ship just as the second torpedo struck and exploded deep within the ship's engine. Suddenly there was no coherent shape that could be called a ship, just three separate parts all disintegrating rapidly as they fell into the planet's atmosphere.

The fourth and last transport engaged its drive and warped out, fully-loaded.

Success!

She felt herself begin to relax. Her fuel gauge began to beep, and moments later her engine died. Four or five other *Hades* fighters were drifting with her.

I'm going to die the true death, but we succeeded! So much sacrifice, but hopefully it will be worth it.

"Attention surviving fighters from the *SCAR*," said the voice over her radio, "the *Hyperion* will take you aboard shortly. Just hang in there!"

She looked over her shoulder. The *Hyperion* was there.

Ron

The gun fired a short, sharp burst upward and pieces of the falling pod exploded like a firework rocket. A thousand glittering fiery little pieces plunged toward the ground, trailing smoke and sparks.

"Beautiful," muttered Chad, "each one of those bastards is just a meat bomb."

He spun the turret twenty degrees to the right, engaged the target-lock, and fired another short burst of needle-pointed rounds into the sky. Another boom and expanding cloud marked the destruction of a second pod.

"Keep it up, soldier," said Ron. Sometime in the last few minutes, the Sergeant-Major and his men disappeared. No sense trying to tell Chad. They had a job to do. *Ironic that the other man truly deserted while they were battling the enemy.*

Chad got two more in the next five minutes, but then nothing. *Maybe the assault was over. Just mop up the survivors and go home.* Ron walked around to the back of the MAC. Both doors there were open. The rear area of the MAC consisted of two benches for soldiers to sit on or stand on as they rode. Nobody was there.

"The other guys bugged out, didn't they sir?"

"Yeah. Not quite sure when."

Ron pulled the doors closed and locked them.

"I can hear more ferals, sir. Sounds like thousands of 'em howling."

"Yeah, let me close these doors and we'll head for the airport."

"Yes sir!"

Ron heard several weapons fire. It was ragged fire, not disciplined. Someone was panicking. He had an idea who.

A doorway linked the rear compartment with both the turret above and the driver's compartment. He climbed through and hoisted himself up into the driver's seat. He could still smell the new leather of the seats. Ron pushed the ignition button. Various systems came online as the engine rumbled to life. There were readouts for engine status, fuel and even the ammo for the auto-cannon. It looked like they were down to roughly two hundred rounds for the cannon, and a third tank of fuel. They could reach the airport no problem, but they wouldn't be shooting many more ferals. He grasped the joysticks, one for each hand, pushed each handle forward, and stepped on the fuel pedal.

The MAC lurched into motion. He made a looping turn by keeping the left handle forward and the right pulled back. They were heading for the airport and coincidently the direction they'd heard the gunfire come from.

They rounded a large rock protruding from the sand and there they were. Three survivors running frantically toward them, followed by a horde of the monsters.

"Mother of God," he heard Chad murmur. "What do we do sir?"

Ron clenched his teeth. One order, and Chad could probably

drop enough of the ferals for the three surviving MPs to reach the MAC and climb aboard. He watched the first, closest man drop, whether from a twisted ankle or what, he didn't know. The other two men ran right past him. Neither had their guns anymore. The ferals were closing in on all three. A few seconds more and none of them would make it.

Ron waited a few seconds more.

The horde reached the fallen man, then the next two.

The feast began.

Ron pulled the left joystick back, the right forward, and hit the gas. They made a wide loping turn around the horde. On the far side they found a dirt track. They turned onto it and followed it all the way to the airport.

Peter

He exited the shuttle, followed by Hatron and the pilot, Ka-Jhea. A few drops of rain fell, mixed in with the grit already blowing in the wind. A small group of people awaited him near the control tower and the huge terminal building complex. He noticed a couple of vehicles. One of them a small tracked military vehicle and the other an ancient ground car painted bright red.

One of the people, a woman, had blonde hair. *Claudia!* Vestiges of human response remained, or maybe he just imagined his blood racing and his heart giving an irregular thump.

He ran across the tarmac shouting her name, as close to alive as he'd ever been once.

Something was wrong.

She wasn't running toward him. If anything, she was shrinking away.

I'm a monster now, he thought.

He slowed to a walk. Noticed the other people waiting, Reaper and a couple of human soldiers, one of them a captain.

"Captain Hoyle, I presume," said the human captain. "I am Captain Ron Davis."

"Nice to meet you, Captain," Peter heard himself answer.

All was ashes now. Claudia was crying but making no effort to come to him.

Someone touched his elbow. The pilot Ka-Jhea. "Be strong, Captain," she whispered.

The human, Davis, was looking him over. Somehow, Peter

kept a straight face.

"What can I do for you Captain Davis?" Peter asked.

Davis smiled. "I was going to ask you the same thing. You see, it appears you are in charge, sir. A naval captain far outranks an army captain. Our president and the entire government didn't make it out of New Charlotte."

Peter made himself stand still, fighting the trembling in his legs.

"You are in charge, sir. What are your orders?"

Peter turned, looking out over the barren dunes. Alpha Centuri Prime was truly a desolate place.

Dead as my heart.

"Gather the troops. We have a capitol to take back."

VISIT US AT

WWW.LIBRARYOFTHELIVINGDEAD.COM

Lightning Source UK Ltd.
Milton Keynes UK
UKOW051840070413

208821UK00008B/219/P